MW01253887

Her Impetuous Rakehell

Aileen Fish

Cover design by Aileen Fish
ISBN 0989568083
Manufactured in the Unites States of America
First Edition May 2015

Acknowledgements

Many thanks go to Vanessa McBride for choosing the name of Louisa's puppy. Your suggestion was exactly the form of torture he needed!

Chapter One

May, 1812
London, England

Laurence Pierce glared at the young man cowering just beyond reach and looked once more at the note the boy had brought. The written words shattered the comfortable world he called his life.

Lord Oakhurst has died. You must see me at your earliest convenience.

His cousin was dead. As Laurence's stomach sank, his hand shook, and he lifted his gaze to the wide-eyed boy waiting to carry a response to his solicitor.

The men at the table where Laurence sat ceased their joking and laughter, setting their cards on the table.

"Is something amiss?" asked Sir Jasper Johnston.

"Quite so." Laurence swiped a hand across his tired eyes. "It would appear I am the new Baron Oakhurst."

Someone coughed. "My condolences."

Amid the murmurs from those around him, Laurence would swear he heard the distinct sound of his cousin's laughter. Yes, it was quite a joke, that he would outlive his cousin. He, who had no property to his name, no one relying on him for an income, and no one to account to but himself. He'd planned to leave his money to his cousin, when the time came. Yet Oakhurst had the nerve to die first.

The lack of sleep from playing cards all night at the club hit him hard. His head was filled with wool and his eyes burned. At least, that's what he blamed it on-the lack of sleep. He stacked his cards neatly on the table in front of him. "Well, lads, I fear I must call it a night. Or a morning."

"You owe me another go," Lord Haymore said gruffly. When the others glared his way, he quickly added, "Another time."

"Yes, another time." Laurence rose and stretched. This nightmare couldn't end soon enough to suit him.

After walking the blocks to his solicitor's office, he stepped inside. A young lady in rather simple gown sat on a bench in the far corner, her arm around a sniffling child. Ignoring them, Laurence approached the neat desk near the door. "Mr. Armistead sent for me," he told the man's secretary.

"Yes, sir, Mr. Pierce. He said to send you right in." The younger man led the way to Armistead's office.

The small room was lined with bookshelves, which, along with the massive carved wooden desk dwarfed the older man. "Do you always keep such early hours?" Laurence sat in one of the chairs.

"And a fine morning to you, too, Pierce. Or should I say Oakhurst?" Armistead was altogether too cheerful for this time of day.

"I really wish you wouldn't. I'm hoping this is all an ill-conceived idea of amusement. Who put you up to it? Lumley? I can see where he'd think this was amusing."

Armistead's face grew somber. "I'm afraid it's true. Lord and Lady Oakhurst were both lost in the uprising in Huddersfield."

Laurence shook his head at the news. "The millworkers who protested the machines. I read about it in the papers. I didn't see Oakhurst mentioned, nor his mill."

"It was one of three burned."

Laurence forked his fingers through his hair. What a horrible end to all the work Oakhurst had put into his business, not to mention the loss of life. "You said Lady Oakhurst died also? What was she doing at the mill?"

"I'm afraid I don't have the details. It would seem Lady Oakhurst left a note with her child's nursemaid with instructions on whom to contact should anything happen. The instructions must have been misconstrued, as the woman arrived here this morning rather than sending someone. We hadn't even had word of your cousin's passing."

"She came here? From Huddersfield? What about the child? Who is caring for her?" The chit must not have the brains of a hen, to take off across the length of England with a child in tow, and no one expecting her visit.

"They are here. You couldn't miss them when you walked in."

"I wasn't aware of my status as a guardian at the time, so I paid them little attention." He'd never met the girl, his cousin's daughter. She must be three or four by now. "What am I to do with her? I know nothing about raising a child. She's too young for school. She should have remained at home. I can't take her to Albany, they'd bar me from the place."

"Shall I enquire into a more suitable home for you?"

"I don't wish to move. I enjoy my life as it is now."

"Your life now includes your ward. There's the Oakhurst estate to think about, as well. I doubt there's enough left of the mill to be concerned with." He cleared his throat and tugged at his cravat. "From what I've read about the uprisings, that is. Horrible thing. With all our soldiers divided between the Peninsula and the Colonies, there is no one to maintain order in our villages."

A heavy lump settled in Laurence's gut. While he wasted his days-and nights-with gaming and horse races, Oakhurst was struggling to keep his business and estate earning some sort of profit. Laurence had tried at times to offer a gift or a loan to help, but his cousin was too proud. He should have done more.

Too late now to help Lord and Lady Oakhurst, but not their child. She deserved better than to be sent back to an empty house to live with servants. His life had been much like that until he'd gone to school, where he met David Lumley and his older brother, Adam, Lord Knightwick. When they went home on holiday, they took Laurence with them to Bridgethorpe Manor. Those were happy times, raising a ruckus, riding horses, swimming in the pond. He smiled just thinking about it.

The decision was easy. He would provide as pleasant a life for his ward as he possibly could. The only question was how he would do so. Oh, and he had one other question. "What is the girl's name?"

"Louisa. Her nursemaid is Molly. They are both quite distressed and quite exhausted."

When their business concluded, Laurence went to speak to his young cousin. He squatted in front of her. Her gown was clean but simple, a plain off-white linen with a pink ribbon tied around her waist. Her wavy red hair was tied at the crown with a matching ribbon, but several locks around her face had come free.

The poor girl snuggled closer to her nursemaid but made no sound.

"Louisa, my name is Laurence. I knew your father and mother. They were lovely people. They have asked me to take care of you, which I will try my best to do."

She peered up at him from behind a lock of hair, but didn't speak.

A single bag sat on the floor beside the bench. Laurence spoke to the maid. "Where are her trunks?"

The wide-eyed, mousy-haired woman shrank back into herself. "I didn't pack any, milord. I feared for our safety and left straight away."

Closing his eyes, Laurence kept his frustration to himself. He had no clue what the pair might have experienced. It would accomplish nothing to make himself a villain from the start. Rising, he held his hand out to the child. "Come then, let us see to your needs."

Louisa hesitated a moment before taking his hand, then walked quietly beside him to the street where he found the hired carriage Armistead had sent for on Laurence's behalf. The only question now was where to take the child.

~*~

Lady Hannah Lumley turned the page of her novel, sitting in the morning room passing the time until Miss Amelia Clawson arrived so the girls could make a few calls on their friends. Mama had rushed off more than an hour ago to Lady Usherwood's bedside, upon hearing her friend had taken ill.

It was difficult for Hannah to keep her mind on the printed words, when there was so much she wished to speak to Amelia about. The Season had just begun, but already she had a handful of young men sending posies each morning following a ball, or inviting her to ride in Hyde Park. She was determined to choose a husband this year. Her sisters, Patience and Madeleine, were eagerly looking forward to their turns in London, and it was a bit much to expect Mama to keep rein on three young ladies.

Not that any of them caused trouble. When they could help it.

She heard a knock at the front door, but it was still to early for Amelia. She guessed it was likely some gentleman leaving his card so he might call later. A moment later, when Coombs entered the morning room, she looked up at the butler in surprise. "Yes?"

"Mr. Pierce is here, my lady."

"None of my brothers are here. Did you tell him to try Knightwick's rooms at Albany?"

"It's Lady Bridgethorpe he wishes to see."

"Mama? Whatever could he want with her?"

"I'm certain I have no guess, my lady."

"Of course not. Where is Mr. Pierce?" She placed a ribbon in the book to mark her page before setting it down.

"In the drawing room, my lady. Shall I send for Nan to join you?"

"There's no need, Coombs. It's only Laurence. He's as close to a brother as any of my own."

Hannah caught the narrowing of eyelids as Coombs showed

his disapproval, and guessed he'd have Nan join her in the drawing room as quickly as possible. Such a fuss over a family friend.

Entering the large room at the front of the house, she saw Laurence standing near the window and broke into a smile. She hadn't seen him since David and Joanna's wedding in March. "I'm so glad you stopped by."

As she cleared the doorway, she noticed the young woman and child seated quietly on the settee. "Hello," Hannah said in their direction. She turned back to Laurence for an introduction.

"Lady Hannah." His slight bow must have been due to the others in the room. Her family had known him so long, no formality was needed. "Is your mother due to return soon?"

He made no mention of the two who had obviously arrived with him. The woman didn't appear to be his type, none of the flash and heavy perfumes he seemed to prefer. She was rather plain, her gown more like a servant's. The child was pretty enough, and her gown was of finer cloth than the woman's. Remembering Laurence's question, she said, "I'm not certain. She is visiting a sick friend."

His lips pressed together and he glanced at the two strangers. "I see. I hoped to seek her advice."

"How unusual. Perhaps I could help?"

"I doubt it. I'm afraid my dilemma is beyond your experience."

Hannah sat in the chair nearest to Laurence and waited for an explanation.

"I received some shocking news this morning."

"That would explain why you are calling so early in the day," she teased. "I don't believe I've ever seen you before four o'clock."

His lips smiled, but the humor didn't spread over his features.

Hannah frowned. Something was wrong. "What has happened?" she asked softly.

"Lord and Lady Oakhurst, have passed away. You see before you the new Baron Oakhurst."

"You?" As the word escaped, she realized how crass that sounded. "Forgive me. I am sorry for your loss. It must be quite a shock for you."

The child uttered a noise somewhere between a hiccup and a cry. "I want my mommy."

Realization hit Hannah and she turned to Laurence for confirmation. "Is this your cousins' daughter?"

He nodded. "Louisa, come meet Lady Hannah."

The little girl looked at the woman beside her before walking closer. She stopped a few feet away and dropped into a practiced curtsy.

Hannah smiled. "I'm very pleased to meet you, Louisa. Miss Pierce, is it?"

"Yes," Laurence said. "Louisa, you may sit down."

"I shall ring for some milk and biscuits," Hannah offered.

"Please don't go to any trouble," Laurence asked.

Glaring at him, Hannah replied pointedly, "It's no trouble. In fact, Louisa, perhaps you'd enjoy playing in the nursery. I'll have one of the footmen show you the way," she added, looking at the woman who must be her nursemaid.

"I won't be staying, my lady," the nursemaid said.

"Oh, well…" Hannah wasn't certain how to respond and turned to Laurence for help.

"That is part of the problem," Laurence began. "Molly wishes to return to her family."

"I can't go back to Oakhurst Castle. I just can't. The men have gone mad. I feared for my life. I'm going back to Cork, where my family is."

"Ah, I see." Now that she looked more closely, Hannah could see the woman wasn't much beyond her own twenty years. It must be difficult to be so far from home. "Did you travel all the way from Oakhurst Castle with Miss Pierce? You both must be exhausted. Why don't I have the cook send breakfast up to the nursery?"

Hannah strode to the hallway in search of a footman. Instructing the first one she found, she sent the nursemaid and Louisa upstairs, then returned to her chair. Laurence took a seat opposite her. "It occurs to me I should call you Lord Oakhurst now."

"I probably won't answer if you do. Can you imagine it? Me, a peer. If ever there was anyone less suited…"

"The papers are filled with *on dits* of lords and ladies who make you seem more like a monk."

Laurence raised an eyebrow.

"Well, that does stretch the truth a little. Of course, I know nothing of your…ah, well, never mind." Warmth washed over her. She and Amelia had spent more than one afternoon discussing the exceedingly handsome Mr. Pierce. She doubted half of what she'd heard was true, but it was so diverting to speak of it. "What will you do with the child? Send her home? Why is she even here in Town?"

He explained what little his solicitor had told him. "And now, with Molly giving her notice, I need a nursemaid as well as a place to live."

"You don't plan to go to Oakhurst Castle?"

He shook his head. "Can you see me wasting away in a country house?"

"But it's a castle! It would be fun to explore it, see what your predecessors have left behind, add some small touches of your own." She secretly hoped the man she married would have an old family home like her father's. She loved the history of it, the connection to the past.

"It's bound to be in a horrid state of disrepair, more likely. I have no desire to oversee such a project. There are much more pressing concerns. Such as, finding a governess."

"She looks about four years old, is that correct? Still too young for a governess. You'll want another nursemaid."

"I'm thinking Louisa might be three. I forgot to ask Molly." He paced a few feet away and turned back. "I have no idea what qualities to look for in a nursemaid. I hoped Lady B would assist me with that."

Hannah laughed at his old nickname for her mother. "Don't let her hear you call her that."

He smiled that way of his that melted the heart of many a lady, young or old. "She enjoys it. She always calls me her dear boy."

"She calls all four of my brothers that. I believe it's to keep from calling one by the wrong name. She'll be happy to help in any way she can. I'll send word to her that she's needed here."

"I don't want to call her away from her visit."

"She'll be glad of the chance to get away. Lady Usherwood has these spells quite often and insists one of her friends stays with her most of the day."

The front door opened and Hannah expected to see Mama. Instead, her brother Knightwick entered. As he passed the open doorway where Hannah and Laurence sat, he stopped and scowled. "What is this about? Pierce, have you lost your head? What are you doing with my sister? Where's Mother? Hannah, where is your maid?"

Before she could speak, Laurence stood and walked to Knightwick. "She is your sister, Knightwick. Nothing untoward is taking place."

"Have you no consideration for her reputation?" Knightwick's scowl darkened. "Anyone could call at this hour and find you here."

"You know I do. I care for her as if she were my own sister. Calm down, man. I was simply waiting for Lady Bridgethorpe to return-"

"And knowing my mother was away, you chose to remain."

Hannah jumped up, putting her fists on her hips. "Really, Adam, you take this too far. Laurence has heard some shocking news and finds himself needing Mama's assistance."

Her brother's features softened when he looked at Hannah. "You are too old to continue to call him that."

"Actually, we must call him Oakhurst now," she replied. When Knightwick's eyebrows drew together, she nodded.

"Forgive me." Adam looked slightly sheepish. "I hadn't heard the news."

"I only learned of it an hour ago, myself. I came here first thing." The line between Laurence's dark eyebrows was the only sign of his distress.

Knightwick clapped a hand on his friend's sleeve. "Any way we might be of assistance, you will let us know."

Chapter Two

When Lady Bridgethorpe arrived a short time later, Laurence rose to greet her. As she handed her bonnet and gloves to a footman she saw the group sitting together. Her warm smile spread. "Mr. Pierce, this is a special treat." She smoothed her graying hair.

"Mama, he's here on grave circumstance," Hannah said.

Lady B grew pale. "It's not David. Or Joanna?"

"No." Laurence rushed to assure her. "My cousin and his wife were lost in the uprisings in Huddersfield. I find myself with a title and a ward."

Raising her fingertips to her lips, her eyes widening, Lady B gasped. "The poor child. Will you go to her?"

"She is here, Mama." Hannah pointed toward the ceiling.

"Ah, I see. Is the young lady resting after her long journey?"

Laurence smiled. "The 'young lady' and her nursemaid are enjoying some biscuits and milk. Their arrival was quite unexpected, and I find myself with no place for them to live." He wasn't going to repeat his refusal to stay at the castle. Lady B had known him since he was a boy. She'd realize how unsuitable that was without his mention.

"I'm happy we may help." Lady B turned to look at her eldest son. "Knightwick, you will have Mr. Soames seek suitable lodging for a small family. In Mayfair, perhaps?"

Laurence nodded. "I've instructed my solicitor to handle that matter, so there's no need for you to trouble yourself. I was hoping you could interview applicants for a nursemaid position. I have no idea what qualities I should look for."

Hannah explained about Molly's desire to return to her family. "I can help you, Mama. You know how I love to study people. I will search out their better qualities and their worst so we might be certain little Louisa has the best of care."

"That sounds delightful. Come, Hannah, we shall send a note to the agency at once." She swept out of the room in her usual grand flurry, the countess in all her glory.

Knightwick remained with Laurence. "Do you think it best to have the girl live under your roof? Wouldn't she be better off in the country?"

Laurence couldn't stop his scowl. "You can't believe I'd be parading my mistresses up the staircase each night. Nor hosting games of cards in my drawing room."

Knightwick chuckled. "No, I suppose not. More to the fact, I've never known you to keep a mistress. I just can't see you caring for a child."

"I've had enough practice with the Lumley brood. Besides, isn't that what a nursemaid is for? My job is to provide a secure home and keep away the rakes when she's old enough to marry."

"It's not quite that simple, although many would say that's enough."

Longing hit Laurence, making a hollow pit in his gut. "I have some memories of my mother singing to me, reading fantastic tales, before she changed. I imagine Lady Oakhurst did the same for Louisa. My father taught me to ride." He smiled and glanced at Knightwick. "I will ask your sister-in-law to take on that duty, as I never learned to ride aside."

Knightwick returned the grin. "Yes, Joanna would be more than suited to the task, although you might ask her to end the lessons before she shows the child how to jump. We'll find you a calm pony when she is ready to learn."

"That seems more a country activity, though." Laurence gritted his teeth. London in the summer was nearly unbearable due to the heat. He only tolerated it because he slept most of the day after being at the club all night. Louisa might prefer to be in the country.

Sleeping all day would be a thing of the past, now. If he continued to do that he might as well send the girl to the castle like an unwanted burden. He closed his eyes for a moment. In no way was he going to let Louisa believe she was a burden. She deserved so much more than the childhood Laurence had had. "I'm not quite certain where she should spend the summer."

Knightwick nodded. "Most of the families will have returned to the country. Is the castle in good repair?"

"I've not been there since before Louisa was born. I imagine money from the mill wasn't enough to keep up with the repairs. I suppose I can send someone to ascertain its suitability. They were residing in it, so it must be livable." He shook his head, again dreading what he feared was the only choice before him. "Can you see me wasting my life away in the north?"

"You never seemed to mind summers at Bridgethorpe Manor when we were young."

"That was different. That's all we had. All we needed. And besides, Cheshire is nowhere near as smoky and, well, industrial as Yorkshire."

"Are you saying you *need* your club and the gaming hells to survive the summer? Again I ask if you believe having that child live with you is wise."

"She isn't 'that child,' she is Louisa. She is family." He sighed as emotions he'd kept buried for many years rose and threatened to close his throat. "She and I are all the family either of us has left. I won't let her feel as lonely as I did at school."

Laurence rose and strode to the window to burn away the uncomfortable feelings inside him. "Your family treated me as one of you, and I will be forever grateful for all you offered me."

"You were another brother as far as we were concerned. What was one more, with all the children running about?"

He was grateful once more for Knightwick's treating the

matter so casually. Knightwick and David were already wild when they'd become friends, playing practical jokes on the field hands or grooms at Bridgethorpe Manor, so Laurence's contributions were probably not even noticed.

"I imagine I'll require your mother's-or Lady Hannah's-assistance often in the weeks to come. There will be clothing to purchase, toys…they arrived with only one small bag for Louisa."

"*My mother* will be happy to help you." Knightwick's emphasis was clear. "My sister is determined to find a suitable husband by the end of the Season, and it appears she's hopeful about one man in particular. Being seen with you won't do her any favors."

Laurence grinned, placing his hand over his heart. "You wound me. You make me sound like some starving wolf eyeing a tasty snack."

"My sister is not a dalliance. Not yours, or any other man. Don't play games with me on this. When it concerns my sisters, I have no humor."

~*~

Mama held up the note she'd written to the light from the window. "I think this will do. Ring for a footman to deliver it, Hannah. I've stressed the urgency in the matter."

Hannah did so, and returned to her seat. "It's a pity Louisa's nursemaid won't stay on at least a little while longer. The child has lost so much, it would be better for her to have something familiar in her life."

"Even if she were still at home, the familiarity wouldn't make up for the fact her parents are missing. Only time will help her adjust to that," Mama said.

"Do you suppose anyone we know has brought their younger children with them to London? Perhaps she can make some friends."

"I can ask Lady Tamwick who she recommends. Or you might take Louisa for a walk in Hyde Park in the morning and see who's about."

Hannah had to smile. Such a silly idea. What was her mother thinking? "I suppose I could ask the nursemaids we encounter whose family the children belong to…"

Mama shook her head. "Oh, dear, I didn't think that through. Well, we'll think of something."

Knightwick entered the morning room where the ladies sat. "Oakhurst will be requesting your help regarding the child's wardrobe and personal things."

"Lord Oakhurst," Mama repeated. "It will take some time to know of whom you speak. He'll always be Laurence to me. I'll be happy to shop for him."

"Oh yes, that will be fun," Hannah added.

"Come to think of it, we probably have some of Lucy-Anne's old gowns tucked away in the attic. We'll have one of the maids search for them."

"There are some dolls and hoops, too, that no one plays with," Hannah said, getting excited about being able to help Louisa cheer up.

"I'm sure Oakhurst will buy what is needed," Knightwick insisted. "Louisa isn't a foundling. At least where money is concerned, she'll be well provided for. I have some business of my own to tend to, but I will be home for supper."

"Should we ask Lord Oakhurst to join us? Perhaps he'll wish to see Louisa before she retires for the night. I assume she'll stay here until he has a suitable home?"

Knightwick nodded. "I've extended the offer for his ward. However, I don't think it wise to have him about while Hannah is here."

Hannah's lips parted in surprise. "He might not be a brother by blood, but everyone knows he is practically family."

Mama laughed. "Knightwick, you sound like your father. Hannah's character won't suffer if we continue our friendship with Laurence."

"You needn't worry," Hannah explained. "I'm certain Lord Downham will be asking for my hand before we leave London next month, and if not him, then Mr. Tatum."

Mama's eyes lit up. "Has Tatum said something to make you think so?"

"Not in so many words, be he's so very attentive, and dances with me every evening."

"There are three or four gentlemen who are attentive. You ride in Hyde Park with a different caller each afternoon. Then there are those who send flowers. You are quite the diamond, my dear girl."

Knightwick slipped away quietly.

Hannah wrapped a stray lock of hair around her finger. "I'm not nearly as pretty as the Sanderson sisters. And Amelia is quite lovely, and she sings beautifully."

"Thankfully there are some young men who haven't gone off to fight the French Menace, so you and your friends will find husbands." Sitting back in her wooden chair, she sighed. "And then I'll have several years at home before we start again with the twins."

Patience and Madeleine were more than anxious to have their Seasons, but at fifteen, they were too young to attend the balls and assemblies. Their family held an annual ball in the local village where all the children were allowed to dance, and for now that would be enough.

The small clock on the mantle chimed. Hannah rose. "Amelia will be here shortly. I must get ready."

Wearing her favorite straw bonnet with the yellow ribbons than matched those on her gown, Hannah waited to speak until she and Amelia were well away from the house, their maids trailing behind them. "You'll never guess the news I have. Mr. Pierce is now Lord Oakhurst."

"No! Will that change his wild ways, do you suppose?"

Hannah held Amelia's gaze for a moment before they both burst out laughing. "I cannot see that ever happening." She sobered when Louisa came to mind. She told her friend about the child. "It makes me so sad to look at her. She rarely smiles unless she in playing with an old doll I found. I believe she's pretending to be her mama."

"I can't imagine losing one's family so young."

"Nor I. Mama will interview nursemaids for Louisa. Oakhurst is looking for a home here in Town where he and Louisa shall live."

Amelia stepped around an older couple walking slowly, then said, "Oh, yes, he can't take the girl to Albany with all the bachelors there. Where is she staying now?"

Hannah explained the rest of the details about the changes in Laurence's life. By then they'd arrived at their first call. Trying hard to remain attentive to their host for the entire fifteen minutes proper manners required them to stay, Hannah found herself studying the other guests in the room. One of the young ladies she knew to have a beau, but the other two hadn't taken anyone's notice. Lady Henrietta Thompson was a sweet girl but not meek, and among the prettiest of the ladies in Town this Season. Her father's estate was said to be penniless, so the only gentlemen likely to consider her were wealthy ones looking to improve their position in Society by associating themselves with a title.

Laurence had his own title now, and he was far beyond wealthy enough to need to consider his bride's income. What he needed was some respectability to improve his reputation in the eyes of the *ton*. Lady Henrietta would be a perfect wife for him.

Hannah said so the moment she and Amelia left.

"Is he looking to marry?"

"No, he is looking for a nursemaid, but what he really needs is a woman to see to his household. He has no experience with running a house. Besides, Louisa is so sweet. She should have a mother to dote on her."

Amelia's eyes narrowed as she studied Hannah. "I can't believe you'd consider any friend of ours to marry that man."

"You don't know him as I do. He's always been so kind to my sisters and me, and mother is quite taken with him. He flirts with her quite shamelessly at times, I admit. He's truly harmless, however. I honestly can't believe why anyone would speak ill of him."

"You sound quite smitten yourself. Perhaps you should

consider becoming Lady Oakhurst."

"I'd sooner marry one of my brothers. He *is* a brother to me. I'd be so pleased if he married one of my friends so I could continue to see him throughout our lives." She burst out laughing. "You should marry him. Then we'd be certain we'll stay close after we leave London."

"We'll always stay friends. However, I might have news of my own about marriage, soon."

"Truly? Mr. Young has spoken to your father? I'm so happy for you."

Amelia looked as if she'd float off like a soap bubble. "He hasn't yet, but I am certain he will."

Hannah wrapped her arms around her friend and squeezed. "I'm so happy for you. I know how much you've feared not finding a husband."

"Papa insists he won't pay for another Season. I was afraid I would have to accept any man who asked, but I'm so lucky that Mr. Young is that man. I can't imagine being happier."

Sighing, Hannah said, "I hope to be as lucky as you. I want to be madly in love with the man I marry."

Chapter Three

Wearing her pale blue gown with silver lace overskirt, her hair plaited with narrow silver lace ribbons, Hannah felt quite the thing at Lady Kettlemore's ball. Apparently Lord Downham agreed, as he'd remained at her side since his arrival, barring the few times he'd danced with other ladies to keep Hannah's reputation out of the scandal broth.

Hannah was too distracted to pay him much attention. In between dance sets, she studied the young ladies in order to make her list of suitable matches for Laurence. She leaned closer to Amelia, who stood beside her with Mr. Young, and pointed with her fan. "Do you know who that lady is? The one dancing with Everton."

Amelia stood on her toes to see around the matron in front of her. "Miss Robb? She is a sweet thing. I don't know if she would be capable of surviving the *on dits* that would come from associating with a rakehell."

"I fear anyone who is able to withstand the stares and whispers will have a legion of titled, wealthy beaux battling over her hand. Mama will have a better chance finding him a nursemaid, I hope."

Lord Downham cleared his throat, holding out his arm. "This is our dance, Lady Hannah." He stood stiffly, as usual, reminding her of a statue. His handsome features were classic, as if he'd been carved by Michelangelo. He was lovely to look at.

"Pardon? Oh, yes, I see they are about to begin." She enjoyed being seen on his arm. She took his elbow and allowed him to lead her into the lines of dancers, where they took their spot. While circling about and crossing over to dance with other gentlemen, Hannah studied the grace of the women dancers, mentally adding a few to her list. So far she had only three names, and two of those were merely somewhat suitable.

"You are very distracted this evening," Downham said.

"I, uh, am considering a new hairstyle and wish to see what the others are wearing. My maid is young and could use some assistance."

"I thought it looked quite lovely this evening. You are a vision, as always."

They separated and Hannah glanced at the ladies watching from the outskirts of the dance floor. That would never do. Laurence needed a desirable match, not one who would otherwise go unnoticed.

The dance steps brought her back to Downham and she made certain she smiled his way. "Did you enjoy your visit to Newmarket? Did you choose the winning horse?"

"I was a fool to wager against a Lumley horse. Your brother's entries are unbeatable."

Pride swept through her in a warm rush. "David does have a good eye for quality." She didn't add how her sister-in-law's training helped. Gentlemen were leery of trusting a woman's touch in such matters, so the Lumleys kept Joanna's efforts to themselves.

When their set of dances ended, Hannah took Downham's arm and looked for Amelia. Had she returned to where their mothers stood?

"Lady Hannah, it's quite warm in here. Perhaps you'd enjoy a stroll outside."

At the recent assemblies, Downham had been increasingly persistent in wanting Hannah to join him somewhere away from the other guests. She knew why. While she'd wondered what his kisses would be like, she wasn't quite ready to find out. Amelia had told her how exciting the first time was, and how the feeling seemed to blossom with each further kiss, but Amelia only had eyes for one man. Hannah hadn't made her final choice yet.

She searched for an excuse. "I had a question for Mama. Perhaps we might wait until later to see the gardens."

Upon reaching her mother, Lord Downham bowed and excused himself, to Hannah's relief. She couldn't think of anything to ask Mama that couldn't wait until the morning. Now she could get back to looking for a bride for Laurence.

Her brother Trey approached, his eyes searching the people around then.

"Whom do you seek?" She asked.

"Hmm?" He jumped, then calmly slicked his hair back with one hand. "No one. I was merely seeing who had come tonight."

She knew better than that. "You know she's smitten with someone."

Trey's smile wavered. "Has an engagement been announced?"

"No. It doesn't matter. She loves someone else, Trey."

He nodded once. "Just so long as she's happy." A few minutes later, he approached a quiet girl standing to one side, and danced the next set with her.

Hannah sighed. She hated seeing her brother so broken hearted. He'd fallen hard and fast for Amelia, who saw him only as the sweet brother of her dear friend. Maybe Hannah should put her scheming toward finding him a wife, and leave Laurence to his own devices.

~*~

Flashing his invitation to Lady Kettlemore's butler, Laurence took in the press of people in front of him on the staircase, all of whom hoped to find enough room to stand inside the ballroom.

What was he thinking in coming here?

A better question was where was the gaming room? That was his sole reason for coming. He'd surprised himself with how seriously he'd considered the propriety of his normal pastimes, now that he had Louisa's future to consider. It made no sense to him that gaming hells were a bad thing, yet playing cards while one's wife or sister danced was acceptable.

That was just one more reason why he avoided Society. They bent their rules to suit their needs. Laurence's opinion was so long as no one was hurt, each man could decide his own limits.

Ignoring the wide-eyed stares of a few of the matrons, Laurence took a spot at the bottom of the staircase. Part of him wished he had the gall to push his way through and go straight to the game room, but he restrained himself.

As he finally neared the top of the staircase, an interminable number of minutes later, the thought occurred to him he should seek out Lady B and say hello before joining the gentlemen. She'd probably enjoy hearing he'd signed the lease on his new home that afternoon.

Yes, an excellent idea to speak with her.

Finding Lady B in the crowd was more difficult than being dealt a winning hand in *vingt-et-un*. He circled the room slowly, pausing here and there to wait for a matron to turn her head so he could be certain of her identity.

He recognized Hannah before seeing her mother. Well, recognized was a relative term. This beauty resembled David's sister, but was much too ladylike, too mature, to be the little girl who'd followed them around endlessly on her father's estate.

Lines of silver ribbons woven through her hair caught the light when she moved her head. Her hairstyle was simple, elegant, allowing her face to shine. Her slender figure somehow demonstrated her gracefulness even as she stood with her friends.

Laurence bristled at the sight of a man eying her in passing. She was too pretty to be there without one of her brothers. Lady B was watchful from a few feet away, but she was no match for some of the men he'd seen in the room. He'd have to speak to Knightwick about the matter, when he saw him next.

Lady B saw Laurence approaching. "Lord Oakhurst, how surprised I am to see you here."

"Not nearly as surprised as I am." He acknowledged the

introduction to Lady B's friend, then made small talk about his search for a home and Lady B's interviews for a nursemaid.

During that time he kept one eye trained on Hannah. When one eye was no longer enough, he excused himself and strolled over to her. "My lady, you are a vision."

She gasped, and a grin lighted her face. "My lord, I'm so pleased you are here."

"Are you? How so? I more expected surprise, as your mother expressed."

"Oh…well…" Her cheeks became decidedly pink. "I think it will be good for Louisa if you raise your standing in Society."

He doubted that was her reason, but couldn't imagine what she might actually be thinking. Before he could press the subject, an older man came to claim her for a dance. Curiosity kept Laurence there, even after she took her place for a second set with yet another man.

It seemed the only way he'd be able to spend a few moments with her would be to dance with her. As soon as she returned, he asked.

"I believe the set before the supper dance is free," she replied.

He bit back a groan. He'd have to wait the entire evening to dance with her. He could go find the cards games until then, but couldn't bring himself to leave her unattended. No matter the room was packed with people. None of them could be trusted to keep her safe.

Lord Downham walked up to Hannah as if they were on quite familiar terms. Laurence's eyes narrowed as he studied the man. Downham was something of a popinjay, and wool-headed when it came to matters of politics or finance. He was lucky to have a title and a profitable estate to cover for the fact he'd probably otherwise be penniless in ten years.

Not only that, there were rumors regarding the seduction of a young lady of large income whose father had ended any hope of the match before the worst could happen.

Laurence stood by Hannah's side, not allowing Downham any

closer. The younger man glared at Laurence.

As Downham opened his mouth to speak, Lady Hannah jumped in. "Do you know Lord Oakhurst?"

"Oakhurst, is it? I hadn't heard."

Laurence nodded, but said nothing. Hopefully the young earl would recognize it for the slight Laurence intended, is spite of the fact Laurence was merely a baron. Maybe then Downham would leave.

Luck wasn't on Laurence's side. Downham turned back to Lady Hannah. "Perhaps we could stroll outside while the musicians are resting?"

Hannah glanced at Laurence, nibbling at her lower lip.

He wasn't about to give her permission, knowing full well what the man had on his mind. What could Downham say outside that he couldn't in here? It obviously wasn't conversation he was hoping for.

She frowned slightly before answering. "Yes."

He watched them go. He couldn't follow them without causing a scene. Not alone, anyhow, but he had a way around that. On his way in, he'd seen the widowed Mrs. Turner, a dear friend who was once something more. They'd continued their friendship after ending their liaison. She'd be happy to see him.

"My dear man!" Mrs. Turner held out her hand. "It has been too long."

"Much too long. If you'd care to walk with me, you may tell me all that has happened since I saw you last."

She fluttered her fan in front of her face, lowering her eyelids seductively. "Well, not *all*…"

He chuckled, and managed to keep his pace casual as he led her toward the open double doors. The terrace, lit by torches, had a wide set of steps leading down to the garden, where glowing lanterns hung from the tree branches. Laurence searched the grounds for Hannah. Only a few couples were visible, so they had to be one of them.

"Laurence, did you hear what I asked?"

He snapped out of his thoughts. "I'm sorry, no."

"I said, the *on dits* is that you have recently acknowledged your... *natural*... child."

Anger soured his gut. "What? Who has said that?"

Mrs. Turner pulled up her sagging gloves. "It's on everyone's lips. Didn't you notice the whispers when you passed through the ballroom?"

"Whispers precede me whenever I attend such an assembly. I care little what is said, most times. But when they suggest my ward is illegitimate, well, they go too far." He wiped his mouth with the back of his gloved hand, wishing it would take away the bitter taste. "She's my cousin's daughter. She cannot be blamed for losing her parents, nor for having one such as me as her only surviving relation. You will do me a kindness if you let it be known she's not my daughter, natural or otherwise."

From the corner of his eye, he saw her studying him, but he paid her no mind. At least, not until she made a pensive sound. "What is it?" he asked.

"You have changed since I last saw you. You've become someone I'd not expected of you."

He sighed. Mrs. Turner was probably the only woman around whom he could be himself completely. "I'm trying. This burden is weighing heavily on me. No, I can't call Louisa a burden. I never want her to hear those words, from me or anyone else. The *responsibility* is unexpected. I'm still trying to determine just what sort of man I need to be."

She patted his sleeve. "Just the sort of man you are. You're so caring and kind, to those you allow close to you. If I'd had children, I'd have no qualms about you being in their lives."

Her words cheered him somewhat. Her belief, and that of Lady B, that he was up to the task of raising a child, let him consider the possibility of truth in the idea.

Ahead on the pathway, under the branches of a tree, Laurence noticed a couple standing quite close to one another. Silver thread in the lady's gown glittered in the light from a nearby lantern. He'd found Hannah.

He hurried his steps. "Why, Lady Hannah, isn't the garden mystical with the hidden lamps?"

Downham stepped back quickly from where he'd trapped Hannah against the trunk.

Hannah looked more relieved than disappointed. "Yes, I was just telling Lord Downham that same thing."

"Would you two care to join us as we continue our walk?" Laurence asked.

"That would be lovely." Hannah stepped out onto the path, forcing Downham to follow. The younger couple led the way.

Mrs. Turner chuckled softly. "Yes, dear man, you have changed."

Suddenly realizing how much so, he almost turned and ran from the place. The thoughts running through his mind scared him witless. He couldn't stand by and let Hannah marry the wrong man. If necessary, he'd step in and offer for her. Well, perhaps he wouldn't act that drastically. He had to agree with Knightwick. Lady Hannah deserved a better man than Laurence. What he could do was make certain she didn't marry the wrong man.

Chapter Four

The next morning, Laurence rose at an hour closer to when he normally went to sleep. His thoughts raced with all he needed to accomplish. His will needed changing first thing. Louisa was now his sole heir. David Lumley was the most suitable person he could think of as guardian, since he was married and settled with his wonderful wife.

As Laurence bathed, he decided he should pay a visit to Louisa. Since he hadn't told Lady B about the home he'd leased, he could accomplish that while he was there. She'd agreed to decorate for him, and he needed to advise her what he'd prefer. Her taste ran toward the classical styles, where he'd prefer something simpler, more masculine.

Once he finished his business with his solicitor, he went straight to Lady B's home. The butler showed him into the drawing room, where, to Laurence's surprise, half a dozen young men stood about conversing with three young ladies, plus Lady Hannah, Lady B, and another matron. Laurence hesitated only a moment before greeting the ladies.

He'd never considered today might be a day Lady B decided to stay home for callers. He supposed that was better than the two being out calling on others. At least this way he could see them both.

Among the men was Downham. Laurence glared in his

direction, his hands tightening into fists at his sides. The man had nerve, playing the gentleman in front of Lady B after nearly seducing Hannah in the garden.

Hannah grinned flirtatiously at Laurence. "I enjoyed dancing with you last night. I had no idea you were so skilled."

He bowed his head. "I've had some practice since Lady B—ridgethorpe," he caught himself, "hired that dance tutor one summer." He glanced at Lady B, whose eyes showed the smile her stern glare couldn't diminish.

"I'm pleased one of you three boys saw some benefit to those lessons," she said. "I fear Knightwick and David prefer to avoid the dance floor."

Lady B then said something to the matron beside her, while Laurence found himself the object of some curious glances by the young ladies, who quickly turned away when he met their gazes.

Hannah must have noticed. "Oh, forgive me. Lord Oakhurst, allow me to introduce Miss Thompson, Lady Marianne Grymes, and of course you know Miss Clawson." She went on to list the young men hovering about. After a pause where no one spoke, she added, "Miss Thompson's father owns Thompson Imports."

Why was Hannah behaving as if he were one of her marriage mart friends? He smiled at the young miss. "I don't believe I've had the pleasure of meeting him."

Another uncomfortable pause, and Laurence spoke. "Lady Hannah, you'll be happy to know I've found a home. Once I furnish it, Louisa and I may move in."

Miss Thompson and Lady Marianne exchanged whispers behind their hands.

Hannah's lips tightened. "Lord Oakhurst intends to raise his ward here in Town, where she may be close to him. I think that's so good of him, when he could have let her remain at her parents' home. Children should know they are loved, don't you think?"

Lady Marianne sniffed. "I agree. We were allowed to visit with our parents every evening."

Hannah offered Laurence a look that clearly said that was the furthest thing from what she'd been thinking.

Laurence waited patiently for the guests to take their leave. Hannah thanked Downham for the posy he'd brought, and Laurence grimaced. Presumptuous twit. Knightwick should warn his sister about men like that who poured on the charm until they seduced a girl, then walked on to the next. Hannah was too sweet, he thought yet again, she needed someone watching out for her.

As soon as the others had gone, Lady B motioned to the chair beside hers. "I am so pleased to see you here today, dear boy. What brings you out for morning calls?"

"To be honest, I hadn't considered you might have guests. I'd hoped to visit Louisa and see how she's adjusting to a new environment."

"How lovely. You'll be pleased to know I've engaged a nursemaid for you. She's to come here tomorrow, so you may make arrangements to let Molly go."

"Excellent." He told her about the house he'd chosen, then rose. "If you'll allow me, I'll go up and see Louisa."

"Of course. If you need anything, please ask."

He thanked her and as he walked out of the room, Hannah joined him and preceded him up the staircase.

"Louisa is such a pitiful thing. She's so sad, but she doesn't cry. All she does is sit in a corner and hug the doll we gave her. I wish I knew what to do to bring her around." She glanced back at Laurence, her concern written on her face.

"Don't expect me to have the answer. Has her nurse had any suggestions?"

"None. She is almost as distressed as Louisa. I hope the new nursemaid has some ideas. Mama said she has a good deal of experience."

He hoped so, too. As much as he'd enjoyed the large family atmosphere at Bridgethorpe Manor, he was more the instigator of the shenanigans than the comforter of ills.

The scene was much as Hannah described when Laurence entered the small nursery. Little Louisa sat on a stool at the lone, large window, a bear wrapped in her arms, staring out the window. He walked to her and knelt on one knee beside her. "Good afternoon, Louisa."

She peered up at him, her eyes rimmed with pink, and dark shadows beneath. "I wish to go home now."

His heart ached and he sighed. "I know. We will have a new home now. New to you and to me. I'm rather uncertain about moving, as I've lived in the same place for many years. Do you think you can help me adjust to a new place?"

"I don't know."

"Perhaps we can help each other. And you may help me choose some toys for you to have in your new nursery."

"Like…a ball?"

"If you'd like. A bear, I think. A doll."

Hannah had been watching them from a distance. "You must have books. Do you like stories, Louisa?"

"I like stories. And biscuits. And a puppy."

"A puppy…" Laurence tossed a warning glance at Hannah. "I don't know if that would be a good idea."

"I want a puppy." Louisa's voice had found some strength.

A strange sound came from Hannah, something like a strangled snort.

Patience. He needed to remember that. "We can discuss that another time. Would you care to play ball with me?"

"No. I want Mama and Papa."

Another snort from behind him. The chit had no sympathy for the child's, or his, position. "I know you do. If I could bring them to you, I would. For now, you must settle for me. Will that be satisfactory?"

"No."

Instead of snorting this time, Hannah came forward. "Change is difficult, isn't it, Louisa? I find myself at a loss at the moment. All of my sisters are at home in the country and I have no one to play with. Would you like to be my friend?"

Louisa considered this, then nodded.

"How lovely. We shall play at my house today, and maybe tomorrow. When you move into your house, I will come play there."

"When will Mama come play?"

A knife lanced through Laurence's heart at the pain the girl must be feeling. "She can't come play anymore, Louisa. She and your Papa had to go to heaven. You have me, now. I know it's not the same, but I hope you will come to be happy in our new life together."

"I want to go to heaven, too."

Laurence pleaded to Hannah with his eyes.

"Your turn will come, but not today. Did Nan bring you some pretty gowns to wear? Let's go see what she found." Hannah held out her hand and Louisa took it, following her to the clothes press in a corner of the room.

Laurence stood and watched in awe as Hannah distracted the child with such ease. Having grown up with so many younger siblings, she had much practice. How many years would it take before it came that naturally to him?

He'd never imagined himself to be in this position. He'd never planned on having a family of his own. As much as he believed Louisa should be raised in a family such as the Lumley's he had no idea how to bring that to her. He'd never felt loved as a child, not from his parents, at least. His mother had died when he was so young, and his father hadn't been the demonstrative sort.

~*~

Hannah held up each of the four gowns so Louisa could see them. "I have some ribbon that will match this one. And some flowers in this rosy shade. We shall buy you a bonnet and I will add them to it. Would you like that?"

"Yes." Her voice was back to the quiet mouse again.

There must be something she could do to cheer the child, some distraction that would make her forget her new circumstances. A thought came to mind but she quickly shot it down. Laurence would never permit Louisa to have a puppy. But it was the perfect remedy to cheer her. Would he allow something smaller, less destructive? She strolled to Laurence. "If a puppy won't suit, what about a k-i-t-t-e-n?"

"A kit—" He stopped, realizing Hannah didn't want little ears to hear the word. "How am I to deal with either of those? Who will feed it, and take it outside? What if a week later she decides she's bored with it and wants a pony, or…an elephant?"

"You may tell her the stable doesn't have a stall big enough for the elephant. But the small animals are little trouble. One of the footmen could add it to his duties, or the nursemaid."

He folded his arms across his chest. "Just how many servants do you suppose I will hire?"

"As many as it takes. How large a house did you lease?"

"As large as it need be."

She smirked. Two could play this game. "Oh, then you'll need many, many servants. Mama will make certain one of them is skilled in the duties a puppy or kitten would require."

"I want a puppy," Louisa reminded them. She'd returned to her stool by the window.

Hannah smirked again, raising an eyebrow in question.

"I'll consider it," he muttered.

A footman stepped into the room. "My lady, her ladyship wishes to speak to you."

"I will leave you two to get better acquainted," she told Laurence, and went down to the sitting room where Mama still sat. "Yes, Mama?"

"Come sit, child."

Hannah took the nearby chair.

"You need to take care. You are too old to continue to treat Lord Oakhurst in such a familiar manner."

"Don't be silly. He is still Laurence, the friend we've known for many years."

"He is Lord Oakhurst, and a rakehell in the eyes of Society, and you are a young lady in search of a husband. What was permissible on our estate is in no way comparable to what your conduct must be here in Town. What will Lord Downham think if he learns you and Oakhurst spend large amounts of time unchaperoned?"

"Molly was there. And I'm not altogether certain I wish to marry Lord Downham. Most days I believe so, but sometimes I feel…uncomfortable around him. I have a few more weeks before I must decide. How can there be anything wrong with my playing with Laurence's ward? She needs a mother's touch." Louisa needed so much more than that, but it was the least Hannah could offer.

"If she needs a *mother's* touch, then *Oakhurst* should consider marrying. How will the child feel when you marry and leave her to establish your own home?"

Hannah hadn't considered that. And Mama's stressing the use of Laurence's title irked her. "You know *Oakhurst* is not the type to marry." She sighed, realizing the truth of what lay ahead for Louisa. "I imagine many children grow up with only a guardian and a governess and they are quite happy."

"We may invite Louisa to visit us in the country. Lucy-Anne is eight years older than she, but she adores children. It would be nice to have a young one around again."

Relief washed over Hannah. "That's a wonderful idea! Perhaps we can take her with us when we leave Town next month."

"We'll worry about that when the time comes. In the meantime, heed my warning. Do not spend time alone with Lord Oakhurst."

Chapter Five

Laurence paused on the staircase when he'd heard Lady B mention his name. So she felt Hannah shouldn't be seen with him, did she? The fact that it might deter Downham from pressing his affections made being seen with Hannah all the better. She said she wasn't certain she wanted to marry the man, so Laurence would be doing her a favor by chasing Downham off.

Yet it might run the others off, too, and Hannah didn't deserve that. While no man was good enough for her, she deserved happiness. Becoming a beloved aunt dependent on her brothers' kindness didn't suit her. She had too much love to offer for that.

How could he scare off one beau while not deterring the others? He'd have to think on that.

When Lady B changed the subject, he continued down the steps. He entered the drawing room pretending he hadn't heard their discussion of him. "Louisa seems to feel somewhat more cheerful. I am forever indebted to you, Lady B, for allowing her to stay here. I won't impose on your kindness much longer."

"Laurence," Hannah said sharply. "You shouldn't call her that."

"Hannah," Lady B sang out in the same tones. "You shouldn't call him that."

The three of them laughed, and he could see Hannah relax into her chair. He hoped his presence didn't cause her distress. When he moved Louisa into his new home, he'd not be calling on Lady

Bridgethorpe as often, so Hannah would have a reprieve.

The thought saddened him. Since David had married, he had little time for Laurence and rarely came to Town. Knightwick was a friend, but they'd never been as close as Laurence and David. Trey had been too far behind them in school to spend much time together, and now spent his time with his studies.

Hannah was the only tie he had to the Lumleys, at least while she was in Town. In a few weeks, she'd return to Cheshire, and possibly marry some time after that. His life had been changing gradually in the last few years, but he'd just passed a sharp fork in the road.

As he rode back to the stable, the entire landscape in front of him became clear. He'd already determined gaming hells must be lower on his list of pastimes, replaced by card games in private residences. How far must he go to appear reputable?

And why had his cousin ever considered him a good candidate for guardian of his only child?

~*~

Against his better judgment, Laurence arrived at the ball Lady Hannah happened to mention when her callers visited earlier that day. He'd play cards at some point, but his main concern was Downham. Since Laurence hadn't spoken to Knightwick, it was up to him to watch over Hannah.

She saw him approaching her in the ballroom and her face shone. "Lord Oakhurst, what a delight." She proceeded to introduce the handful of wallflowers who stood with her.

He offered them a bow. Addressing Hannah, he asked, "Do you have a free dance this evening?"

"I do. I believe we all do," she added with a wicked grin, glancing at her friends.

"Lovely." Dear Lord, this was going to be a long night. Saucy chit, she was.

She had the nerve to look smug. "Lady Henrietta has this next dance free."

The others dancers were moving toward the center of the

room. He offered his arm to Lady Henrietta. "Shall we?"

He maneuvered to line up next to Hannah's partner. He kept up the expected dialogue with his partner, but let Hannah know with his eyes that she could expect retribution for her little matchmaker ploy.

Hannah made him dance with each of her four friends before admitting to having a free dance of her own. When that turned out to be a waltz, his frustration eased. Her grin was quite flirtatious as she nibbled her lip. Where had she learned to taunt a man that way? Did she have any idea how that affected a man?

"You appear to be enjoying yourself," he said.

"I adore dancing. I would do so every night if I could."

"My feet wouldn't stand for it, so to speak, if I tried. These dance pumps aren't the least bit comfortable."

"They fit better with some wear." As she circled around the next dancer in line, she glanced at him from the corner of her eye. "This is only the second assembly I recall seeing you attend."

"I've had the shoes for several years."

"Yet you've only attended a ball in recent days." Her look became more serious when they again met in the center of the two lines of dancers. "Is it Louisa? You're not—"

They parted again and he wondered what she'd been about to say.

~*~

The oddest thought struck Hannah. There was only one reason Laurence would suddenly appear at assemblies on a frequent basis. The same reason the others were there. He'd decided to find a wife.

Since she'd already determined to help him with just that, the idea he was a willing participant should please her greatly. Yet it had the opposite affect.

What had been a game now could become real. How silly of her. It *should* become real. Even Mama had said so. Louisa deserved a family. Laurence's marriage would mean Hannah's family would see less of him, but her own marriage, whenever it happened, would mean she saw less of both Laurence and her family.

She'd mentioned the same thing to Amelia, but she and Amelia could easily visit each other at their new homes. Unless Laurence married one of her close friends, she'd only see him when she and her husband came to Town and happened upon Laurence and his wife.

She hadn't known anyone as long as she'd known Laurence, except for their neighbor Jane, who'd married their cousin Stephen. The couple now lived near enough to Bridgethorpe Manor to visit often. The prospect of losing Laurence's company sat heavy on her.

The dance ended and Laurence paused before her taking her back to Lady B. "Are you unwell?"

"I am quite well. Perhaps I've had too much dancing, as have your poor feet."

"I'll bring you some lemonade."

"I would enjoy that," she said. "Thank you."

~*~

When Laurence returned with the two glasses of lemonade, Hannah was deep in conversation with Downham. With indescribable glee, Laurence held out a glass to Hannah. "Your refreshment."

Downham's eyes narrowed, but he said nothing.

"Thank you," Hannah said.

As if Downham's presence wasn't bad enough, George Tatum appeared, bowing gallantly before Hannah. "My dance is about to begin."

Downham's scowl deepened. Hannah gracefully handed Laurence her glass, accepted her escort's arm and disappeared in the crowd.

Lady Hannah was so small Laurence couldn't see her through the taller men and ladies standing between them. He knew Tatum couldn't attempt anything untoward with so many people watching, but an irrational angst ate at him. Laurence was quite tall, and if he couldn't see Hannah, it was certain her mother couldn't. Tatum could convince Hannah to slip away to some alcove, or out in the garden as Downham had done. Someone needed to watch over her, and he was the only one in a position to do so.

Lady Henrietta stood hidden behind a Greek column, either pushed there by the crowd or hoping to not be seen. She would be the perfect accomplice, provided he only danced one more time with her. He might not attend balls on a regular basis, but he knew the implication of singling a lady out for more than two dances. "Lady Henrietta, would you do me the kindness of partnering with me?"

She blinked, expressionless, then the smallest smile broke through. "Yes, thank you."

The music had just begun, so he practically dragged the poor girl into place. She didn't appear any more comfortable opposite him than she had the first time. He felt sorry for her. "Have you and Lady Hannah been friends long?"

"Our mothers have been close friends since their own Seasons."

Armed with that information, he realized he could have chosen a better partner. Lady B might think it the perfect situation for him to marry her dear friend's daughter. He was tempted was to question his future dance partners on the depth of their acquaintance with the Lumleys, prior to asking them to dance.

Lady Henrietta was, however, just the person to pass along some useful information. If she knew Hannah was close to choosing the wrong man, Laurence could pass the information to Knightwick. "You and Lady Hannah must be quite the confidants. Do you exchange secrets?"

She blushed, making him wonder just how detailed their conversations might be. "I suppose so. I don't know that I'd call them secrets, though."

Excellent. "I'm told all young ladies enjoy comparing the qualities of the gentlemen who are said to be ready to marry that Season. Does Lady Hannah have a favorite?"

She hesitated, so he added, "I'm a close friend of the family. You may tell me anything without fear. I'm tight-lipped and would never let the secret go any further."

"Well, she believes Lord Downham will make her an offer

soon."

"Has she said how she feels about this?"

The dance steps separated them. When she drew near again, she said, "She…to be honest, Lord Oakhurst, I don't feel comfortable discussing my friend this way."

"I understand." He gave her credit. Too many people were all to eager to blurt everything they knew or had heard about another person, no matter the level of their friendship. Yet if Lady Henrietta thought there was nothing between Hannah and Downham, she would most likely have said so.

The question was how to discourage Downham. Short of inviting the man to meet him in the ring in Gentleman John's Saloon for a few rounds of boxing, Laurence couldn't think of any action pointed enough to make a sound impression. Fighting her beau was hardly the way to convince Hannah he had her best interests at heart.

The alternative would be to appear to be considering her himself, but he'd never mislead her that way. Regardless of his visions for a warm family life with Louisa, he couldn't bring himself to pretend to consider some girl for his wife. That would be the cruelest thing ever, not only discouraging another man but also doing the very deed he accused that man of attempting.

He needed Knightwick's help.

First, since he was making a second round of dances with her friends, he could ask Hannah to dance again. As soon as he'd returned Lady Henrietta to her mother's side, in the small group that included Hannah and Lady B, he did just that. "I'd be delighted if you'll stand up with me again, Lady Hannah."

Lady B's reaction was confusing. Her forehead furrowed and she narrowed her gaze at Laurence. "Hannah, you've promised the remaining sets this evening, haven't you?"

"No, I do have another dance free, after Mr. Tatum's second. Lord Oakhurst, I shall save it for you." Her eyes sparkled. Was she more pleased that she'd vexed her mother or that she'd dance with him again?

He remained with Lady B and Mrs. Thompson while Hannah and Lady Henrietta danced with their partners. Lady B wrapped her hand around his arm. "Let's take a turn about the room, dear boy. I am weary of standing still."

He patted her fingers, leading her through the press of the crowd. "I could lead you out in the dance after Hannah's, if you'd prefer."

She chuckled. "I do hope you are not using your skills on my daughter."

"My skills?"

"Your ease of flirtatious conversation worries me. Your reputation concerns me." She paused to greet a friend, then they walked on. "I understand the relationship between you two, but most of Society would prefer to think the worst. You don't do her any favors by singling her out for your attentions."

He parted his lips to point out how he'd danced twice with one other young lady just a short time before, but he knew that wasn't what she meant. She saw through his words, even when he tried to fool himself. "I mean her no harm. I enjoy her company, however, and worry about some of the men who are spending a lot of time with her."

"Any gentleman in particular? Is there something I should be aware of?"

He led her into an alcove where they might speak more privately. "You can't have missed the rumors surrounding Downham."

"What people infer and the truth rarely interlace. You, of all people, should know that."

He couldn't stop himself. He grinned. "Can you be certain where the line was crossed?"

Her stern frown returned.

Laurence sighed. "You are correct. Rumor greatly exaggerates fact, and sometimes creates a world unto itself. But I've heard directly from one girl's brother regarding implied promises of marriage that never materialized. Lady Hannah is important to me. I don't want to see her hurt."

"You surprise me. Before Louisa came into your life you demonstrated no hint that you were concerned about others."

Those words sliced sharply through him. "Was I really so shallow?"

She patted his arm. "I wouldn't call you shallow, even in your most devious moments. You've never spoken of apprehension over anyone's future, though, at least in my presence."

That was true, but David was the only friend who'd married recently, and his choice in a bride had been perfect for him. Laurence had questioned his sanity in thinking of marriage so young, but the lady he'd chosen had the ideal qualities suited to David's lifestyle. "I had my moments with David, but he's much more likely to listen to reason than Lady Hannah would."

"Yes, it's not your place to warn Hannah. I would appreciate if you brought your concerns to me. And please, don't be so public with your friendship with her. It's likely to be misconstrued."

Chapter Six

A few days later, Hannah woke early, unable to sleep in her excitement. Laurence had signed the lease on his house, and had asked Mama for assistance furnishing it. Hannah enjoyed helping Mama choose wallpapers and carpets when she redecorated, but the idea of selecting the furniture itself was too grand to imagine.

When she married, her husband would most likely have a home that was decorated to his taste, or filled with family pieces. He might allow her to change a few small things. Laurence, however, needed everything. From nutmeg graters in the kitchen to a backgammon table, his purchases needed to be of a style suited to his new rank in Society.

Mama met her at the breakfast table, where Hannah had nearly finished her toast. "What has you so bright-eyed at this hour?"

"You well know. We are helping Oakhurst today." She hoped Mama caught her proper usage of his title, even though they were alone in their dining room.

"'We?'"

"Oh, you must let me accompany you. You know how I love matching curtains to carpets and upholstery. I have no engagements today." She held her breath awaiting the answer.

"What will people think? I'm beginning to believe you have no care about finding a husband. If that is the case, why are we here? I'd much rather be at home caring for your father."

Hannah sat back as guilt filled her. "Is it really so awful here? I thought you enjoyed the assemblies and seeing your friends."

"I do, my dear, but we are in Town for a specific reason. If anyone sees you shopping for furnishings with any man, they'll be watching for the banns to be read. We both know Oakhurst has no plans to marry, at least not soon, so if you'd set your sights there, you'll end up heartbroken."

Laughing, Hannah said, "How can you imagine such a thing? He is my dearest male friend, but that is all. If Jane or Joanna were here, they'd offer to shop also."

"Yes, but they are married." Mama waited for the footman to set her plate in place and walk from the room before she continued. "I've seen the looks exchanged between Oakhurst and Downham. Lord Downham obviously feels Oakhurst is his competition. If he feels so, what must the rest of the *ton* be thinking?"

"I will explain my relationship with Oakhurst to Downham."

Mama choked on her coffee. "You'll do no such thing! You won't discuss Oakhurst with anyone, except your female friends, should they develop a fondness for him, and then only to warn them away."

Hannah shook her head. "He's not so bad a man as to deserve that. He deserves a respectable wife, one who will love him for who he is, not his income. I know he can't have done any of what the gossips say about him. If he was seen with all those ladies, whether widows or not, it was likely he wished to avoid the appearance that he favored the company of one woman."

Mama did not look convinced, but rather a touch disbelieving. "I do hope you don't discuss such things among your friends."

Hannah avoided her mother's gaze hoping not to reveal anything. "I only speak on the topics my friends enjoy."

"It hasn't been so long since I was your age. I hope when you bring up a man's…social habits, you are not in danger of being overheard."

"We are very discreet, Mama. Never fear."

"I still believe helping Oakhurst shop would be ill advised. I won't allow it."

~*~

After a day of following Lady B around one of the finer emporiums in London, Laurence was certain his home couldn't contain that much furniture. Still, the styles suited him, the wallpapers not overwhelmingly old-fashioned or feminine.

He'd been disappointed that Hannah hadn't joined them, as he valued her opinion. Most likely Lady B was doing her best to keep them apart. He wasn't going to thwart the woman's efforts to keep her daughter's image as pure as Society demanded. The idea his presence alone could tarnish Hannah's future irked him, but arguing the matter did no good.

The next day seemed perfect for being outside, ideal for taking Louisa on an outing. He'd noticed an advertisement in the paper of a marionette act in the park that afternoon. He quickly penned a note inviting Lady B and Hannah to join them, and called for his footman to deliver the message.

A small doubt lingered that Lady B would allow to let Hannah go along. She'd made excuses yesterday regarding Hannah's prior engagement and had helped him shop on her own. He was growing tired of her interference. The more she pushed him away, the more he wanted to spend time with Hannah.

Her dry wit and unrestrained laughter were such a pleasure after the polite twitters from "proper" ladies, although in some that term might refer to their public appearance, not their general behavior. From the time she began to wear her hair up he'd known Hannah's beauty would make her quite popular among the *ton*, but when she dressed for an evening out, some magic was performed that singled her out in even the largest gathering.

None of the men she appeared to be considering were good enough for her. He gritted his teeth. He couldn't think of any man worthy of her. No matter whom she married, she'd be settling for a man who was beneath her.

His footman returned with Lady B's answer. They'd be happy to join him and Louisa on his outing. Laurence was pleased to arrive at their home in his new barouche-landau, complete with two matching bays and a coachman.

A house, a carriage large enough for a small family, people under his employ- what was happening to him? Just months ago he was happily unencumbered, sharing a valet with several of the bachelors at the Albany. He didn't regret the addition of little Louisa to his life, but he-anyone who knew him, for that matter-would never have believed him capable of adjusting to these changes.

Louisa looked leery about leaving Lady B's home with Laurence, but she happily took Hannah's hand and climbed into the carriage, leaning over the side to look down at the street. "It's broken."

"What's broken?" he asked, sitting beside her, their backs to the horses.

"The carriage. The top broke off."

He chuckled. Her father could likely only afford one carriage, if that, a very serviceable one. "The top is merely pulled down." He tugged her bonnet so it hung down her back. "Like your bonnet," he added.

A pout clouded her cheerful face and he feared she was going to cry.

Hannah laughed brightly and tugged at the ribbons holding her own hat in place. "How fun, to let the wind blow in your hair, don't you think, Louisa?" She nodded sharply at her mother.

Lady B frowned. "You'll turn brown, my dear. You're determined to vex me, aren't you?"

"Oh, mama, one outing without a hat won't ruin me."

Turning her glare on Laurence, Lady B simply responded, "We'll discuss it later."

An odd form of tension had simmered between mother and daughter recently. He hoped he wasn't the cause of it. Rather than continue to cause strife, he untied Louisa's bonnet and replaced it on her head. Due to the angle he was sitting, he had difficulty tying the ribbons beneath her chin. The resulting bow ended up slightly askew, but he knew no one would comment on it.

Louisa yanked at the ribbons, untying them. "It's crooked. The bow goes here." She pointed beneath her chin.

Drawing in a deep breath, Laurence forced a cheerful smile. "I need practice, and I see you will give me much of it until I get this right. Please turn toward me so I may do this properly." He refused to glance at the two ladies opposite him, knowing they must be laughing at his situation.

With the bow tied, he sat back and took in the passing scenery, intent on keeping his mask of composure in place. He couldn't let them see how close he was to losing his weak grasp on the life he now found himself living. If someone had pulled the carpet from beneath his feet he couldn't have been more off balance.

"Has David mentioned the filly he's looking to acquire? Colonel Sir Lewis Branson's horse out of Zephyr's granddaughter." Somehow in recent years Hannah had become a skilled conversationalist, gracefully guiding them into safer territory.

"No, I hadn't heard. Your father must be overjoyed at the news."

"They haven't mentioned it to him yet. David and Knightwick don't wish to get his hopes up and have it come to naught."

"That's probably for the best."

"Yes."

Lady Bridgethorpe's hands had come together in a firm grasp at the mention of the earl. She never spoke of it, but her husband's prolonged illness must weigh heavily on her. One would never know it to see her in Society. She kept up a strong front.

"We're planning a celebration dinner when Trey finishes his studies. We haven't set a date yet, but it will be before Mama and I return to the country. You must plan on attending, as you are practically one of the family." Hannah paused a moment before adding, "Isn't that right, Mama?"

Lady B's smile appeared genuine enough. "Of course, Laurence. You will come, won't you? My younger three daughters will attend, and Lord Bridgethorpe, if he's strong enough."

"It sounds delightful. I will be sure to come." He returned

to watching the passing traffic, his thoughts going back to his surprise at Lady B's acceptance of his invitation. Against his better judgment, he mentioned it. "I wasn't certain you'd both be able to join Louisa and I this afternoon."

Hannah glanced at her mother, but kept quiet.

Lady B narrowed her gaze. "It's important that Louisa have some female company in addition to her nurse. I don't think it wise we make a habit of being seen together in Society too often, you understand. After you are settled in your new home, it would be better for you to have Louisa's nursemaid bring her to our house."

He nodded. "I see. And I understand your meaning. I only considered making the child more relaxed in my presence, and having you two, with whom she's grown familiar, join us improves her enjoyment."

"Are you enjoying your outing, Louisa?" Lady B's expression softened as she looked at the young girl.

"Yes, ma'am."

"Have you seen marionettes before?" Hannah asked.

"What's a mary-nette?"

Laurence sat back and let the ladies talk to Louisa for the rest of the ride. She grew more animated the more she spoke, and by the time they reached the park she jumped from the carriage step onto the street. He offered a hand to Lady B and Hannah as they stepped down, then gave his arm to Lady B to lead them into the park.

Louisa ran ahead of her nursemaid, looking more like a four-year-old than he recalled since her arrival in London. Hannah hurried to catch up with them, leaving Laurence to walk with the countess.

"How is she faring?" he asked.

"As well as can be expected, I imagine," Lady B answered.

"I'm unfamiliar with the behavior of children, especially not one who's lost as much as she has."

"Tell me, dear boy, do you plan to bring a mother into her life?"

He gnawed the inside of his lip. Lady B was the one person who could see beyond his fibs, so there was no hope of lying to her. "I won't marry for the sake of Louisa alone. That isn't the life I want to give her."

"Perhaps you should be using your evenings wisely and getting to know the young ladies who are still free to choose among."

He grew tired of these veiled inferences to avoiding Hannah in public. "I'm not comfortable with the small talk expected of me. I don't like the idea of raising the hopes of every young woman I asked to dance."

"I could put in a good word with a few matrons who plan an afternoon of cards or a poetry reading, or a musicale. I know how you love your cards."

He chuckled. "Can you see me sitting through recitations of poetry? I never cared much for reading, and listening to someone do so poorly is the worst torture I can imagine."

"Oh, I could introduce you to forms of torture you've never considered." She patted his arm. "It's lucky I love you, Lord Oakhurst. As long as you behave, I won't subject you to my humor."

"I consider myself forewarned."

They reached the gathering of children, most with a governess or nursemaid watching over them. The puppeteers kept the children laughing with a nonsensical skit. Hearing Louisa's laughter warmed him, wiping away all the ill feelings Lady B's warnings stirred in him.

When the show finished, Hannah took Louisa's hand and they walked together down the path, the nursemaid a few paces behind. Laurence and the countess followed. Suddenly, a brown-spotted spaniel puppy darted across the path.

"Puppy!" Louisa squealed.

Hannah held her back. "It's not our puppy, honey. It's dirty. Let's leave it alone."

"I want a puppy!"

"Maybe one day Lord Oakhurst will let you have one."

Laurence cringed. The words made him sound callous. He

wasn't a heartless man simply because he didn't want the dirt and hair, not to mention the noise, of a dog in his home.

Kneeling, Louisa broke into fits of giggles when the pup stretched on its hind legs to lick her face. The child squeezed it, sheer joy all over her face.

Lady B said nothing, but looked up at him expectantly.

He shook his head. "It's filthy. Most likely flea-ridden. It must belong to someone."

"It doesn't appear to be well-cared for. It's awfully thin," Hannah said.

"A dog should be able to hunt, or herd, or guard, or something. This scrawny thing doesn't look capable of any of that."

"No," Lady B said, "but it seems terribly good at loving Louisa. That *is* a job you need filled at this time."

She didn't say the next few words he expected, but he knew she felt the same thing he did. He would be taking home the dog. "Very well. I'll have one of the servants bathe it and make it a bed belowstairs."

Louisa clapped her hands. "Thank you!"

Hannah picked up the squirming bundle of fleas and cockleburs and pressed a hand against its muzzle to keep it from licking her chin. "Well then, what shall we call it?"

"Lulu," Louisa shouted.

"Is it a male or female?" Lady B asked.

Hannah held the dog at arm's length. "It's a male. Louisa, we need a boy's name."

"I want to call it Lulu."

"I can't have a dog named Lulu, no matter what sex," Laurence muttered.

"What about Spot? Harry? Laury?" Hannah smirked at Laurence as she said the last one.

"Lulu," Louisa insisted.

Hannah raised an eyebrow at him.

He sighed. This had better not be a sign of things to come. "He'll be called Lulu, then."

Chapter Seven

Hannah glided around the floor in Mrs. Helmsley's ballroom, in the arms of Lord Downham. She loved waltzing more than anything she could think of, at the moment. The graceful movements, the gentle music, and the scent of Downham's cologne filled her senses.

"What has you so deep in thought?" Lord Downham asked.

"No thoughts, actually. I'm simply enjoying the moment."

"That pleases me. I enjoy seeing you so happy." His eyes smoldered with what she hoped was love. "My wish is that you always feel thus."

Always. Was that a hint? There was only one way he could ensure her future happiness, and that was to marry her. Butterflies fluttered inside her. Why did he wait so long to say what she longed to hear? If he preferred to seek permission first, he could speak to Knightwick. He stood in their father's stead more often than not, now. Knightwick's approval would be accepted by her family.

Amelia waltzed past simply aglow in her pale blue gown. Mr. Young had a pinched look, as if his shoes were too tight, or he had something worrisome on his mind.

Hannah gasped. Was tonight the night Mr. Young would propose? How lucky her friend was to finally have the mattered settled, and what's more, to marry the man of her choosing.

Lord Downham's lips turned down. "I see Lord Oakhurst is

here. He's been attending a surprising numbers of assemblies of late. I wonder what his purpose is."

"He told my mother he wishes to improve his reputation so as not to disparage that of his ward as she matures."

"Humph. I can't see him doing something as honorable as that."

The hairs on the back of her neck bristled. He might as well speak poorly of one of her brothers. "If you believe that, you do not know him as we do. He's a very kind and generous man. I've known him most of my life."

Downham looked down his nose at her. "I'm astonished your parents allow you to associate with the man."

She bit her tongue. She wouldn't rise to argue with him. This was a side of him that caused concern. He couldn't object to Laurence's presence when her family gathered, but his superior attitude was not something she could endure for a lifetime. He'd appeared haughty at times, which she could understand as an earl's heir, but never so condescending as when he spoke of Laurence.

What had happened between the two men to give him such a disliking for Laurence?

Their waltz ended and Hannah was glad to let him walk away to play cards until time for their next dance. Mr. Young brought Amelia to stand beside Hannah, and took his leave also.

"I'm so excited," Amelia said, her grin spreading.

"Has he said anything?"

"He asked permission to call on me tomorrow." She grasped Hannah's hand. "I think he will propose."

Hannah hugged her friend. "I'm so happy for you. I knew he would eventually, but to keep you waiting after his marked attention last Season, well, it's simply callous. But he's making up for it now."

"I didn't know it was possible to be so happy."

"You deserve it more than most. You two will be so good to each other." As happy as she was for Amelia, Hannah hoped her own situation would be resolved soon. This waiting was unbearable. What more did he need to know of her character to decide she was a good match? He must know by now if he was capable of loving her. Her income was not meager, and he didn't appear to be in financial straits, so he wouldn't be waiting for a lady with a large income. Rarely did she feel insecure about anything, but those doubts arose now. "Do you think Downham cares for me, Amelia?"

"Of course he does," she answered. "He favors you over any of the other ladies at balls. He never dances with anyone else more than once and always dances twice with you."

"That's true. And he compliments me often. Yet he doesn't look upon me the way your Mr. Young does." Hannah had been so certain of his growing love for her just a month ago, but as the time grew closer to the highly anticipated proposal, her doubts had begun to take root. If only he'd speak up before those doubts blossomed.

After their next set on the dance floor, Lord Downham stopped before they had returned to where Mama sat. He leaned close and spoke in her ear. "Come find me in ten minutes. I will be in the fourth door beyond the ladies withdrawing room." As he straightened, his smile sent shivers down Hannah's spine and a wave of warmth up her neck.

Lord Downham wanted to see her alone. This must be the moment she was waiting for. He was going to propose.

~*~

Laurence no longer heard what the man next to him was saying. Downham had whispered something to Hannah that made her blush brightly. Then the man walked away, weaving his way through the crowded room and out the doors. A voice in Laurence's head told him something was wrong. "Excuse me, gentlemen. Enjoy your evening."

Striding as quickly as he could without jostling people aside, Laurence followed the earl into the hallway. In one direction candles lined the walls, but the other direction was dark. A door opened near the end of that hallway, casting light in the darkness, enough to see Downham slip inside and shut the door behind him.

The hairs on the back of Laurence's neck prickled. He checked to make certain no one paid any attention and he continued down the hall. A door to his left stood open, the room inside dark, so he stepped within to wait. Only a short time later he heard light footfalls drawing closer. He peered around the doorway.

In the light from the opposite hall, he could make out Hannah's features. He quickly grabbed her arm, slipped a hand over her mouth to cover her gasp of surprise, and pulled her into the room. He shut the door quietly behind him.

Hannah pounded a fist on his chest. "You frightened me! What are you about?"

"I'm more concerned about what you are up to. Please tell me you took a wrong turn. The withdrawing rooms and the card room are in the other direction."

She turned away as if he could see her expression. The act alone confirmed what he feared. She'd been planning to join Downham. Hannah moved toward the window where the moon shone brightly. Tugging on a pale ringlet, she said, "I was merely escaping the heat and the noise of the ballroom. What on earth are you doing, sitting here in the dark?"

He wasn't about to admit to it. "The same. I happened to notice an acquaintance of yours had also left the festivities."

She turned her head to stare out the window. "Really? Who might that be?"

Laurence closed the distance between them, stopping near enough he could feel the heat from her body. Her lilac perfume drifted up to him, the scent calming some of the anger he'd felt when he entered the room. "Your friend, Lord Downham."

"Oh, I thought he'd gone to play cards."

"Your mother has warned you about meeting with men alone, hasn't she?"

"Do you mean as we are now?"

"You know very well what I mean, Hannah. Men like Downham will take advantage of you more quickly than you can say 'boo.'"

Especially when they stood so close to a beautiful young woman with such a graceful neck and subtle scent. The temptation was too great for most men. Thank goodness she was like family to him.

"I'll have you know he was going to propose to me," she argued.

"Did he say so directly? In that case, I apologize for thinking so little of him. He's spoken to Knightwick already, has he?"

She ducked her head. "If he has, neither Knightwick nor Mama has mentioned it. Perhaps he wished to make certain I'd accept before seeking permission."

"Or perhaps he had other motives for encouraging you to leave your mother's side."

Hannah spun and faced him, her features in shadow. "You, of all men, should know how a man behaves. You've never had an assignation at a ball, is that what you're trying to tell me? You didn't gain your reputation as a rakehell through paying morning calls."

His eyebrow raised. "Is that where you were heading? For an assignation? I should drag you back to Lady B's side and tell her never to let you out of her sight."

"Oooh, that isn't what I meant. I told you he only wished to propose to me."

"A proposal can be done in a lady's drawing room. You can't be so trusting. Men like Downham will take more than kisses and lose interest once they've had what they want."

She folded her arms across her chest. "You know nothing about men who are planning to marry. You think they are all like you and wish to flit from lady to lady."

"Is that what you think of me?" He had difficulty keeping his voice low enough to not be discovered. "Be honest with me, Hannah. Just because I haven't looked to take a wife, you believe I'm taking advantage of half the *ton*?"

Peering up at him, Hannah shook her head. The ringlets around her face bounced. "I know you better than that. I'm simply angry with you for treating my like a child. "I'm twenty years old now, old enough to take care of myself."

"Age and innocence don't grow equally. I pray you never lose your innocence."

"I'm tired of waiting. I want to kiss a man. Amelia tells me it's the most wondrous thing, and after two Seasons I only have her word on it. I admit it—I'd hoped Downham would kiss me after he proposed. Is it so shocking to want a kiss?"

"If it stopped with a kiss, no, it wouldn't be scandalous, but I doubt he would have stopped there."

Hannah grunted. "All men aren't like you, Laurence."

She thought he had no self-control. She had no idea the control he maintained a the moment. She wanted a kiss, did she? And she didn't think he could stop with just one? The girl was playing with fire and had no notion of the fact.

"Don't push me, Hannah."

"See you admit as much. Let me pass. Let me go speak to Lord Downham."

If he let her walk away now she'd go straight to the earl and most likely demand a kiss, simply to prove she could. Laurence couldn't bear the idea.

Before he could think it through, he gasped her shoulders and pulled her to him, pressing his lips to hers. He sensed her gasp, felt the softening of her lips just before she leaned into him. Her hands were pressed against his chest but not pushing him away. His own tension slipped away as he brought his hand up to cup the back of her head.

Sanity caught up with him. What was he doing? He stepped back abruptly but couldn't bring himself to apologize. The look she gave him made his gut drop. Confusion, questions… He should be seeing shock, anger. She should slap him, pound on his chest for being so rude, so unforgivably brazen.

He wanted to hug her, to take it back.

Visions of her continuing down the hall to meet that whoreson crept back into his thoughts, annihilating any trace of guilt Laurence felt. He gently brushed his thumb over Hannah's lower lip. "Now you will have that between you and any other man who tries to kiss you."

He turned and left the room before he kissed her again.

~*~

Hannah's fingertips traced over the skin where Laurence's thumb had stroked her lip. A kiss was nothing like Amelia had described it. Exciting was too pale a word to communicate all the sensations that had rushed through her body. The butterflies, the melting of her bones to the point she thought she'd end up a puddle at Laurence's feet.

The hunger for something she didn't really understand.

If he'd tried to do anything more to her she wouldn't have stopped him. Now she understood why everyone worked so hard to keep young people apart. How easily she'd lost the desire to remain proper.

Would she feel the same after a kiss from Lord Downham?

At the moment, Hannah didn't care to find out. She didn't want to share this feeling with anyone else, not even the man she hoped to marry. She didn't care if that made her wicked and undeserving of a good husband. As she lay on her pillow tonight, she'd run through the kiss in her mind, savor every moment of it, then tuck it away so tomorrow she could waken with a clear mind.

Chapter Eight

Laurence woke to screams and sharp yapping, and thunder like no little feet could possible produce. His heart pounded until he realized those were happy noises. He reached for his pocket watch on the table beside his bed. Ten o'clock. At this hour the only noise that made him happy was the sound of his own snores.

He yawned and rubbed his eyes. As he did, his actions of the night before came back to him. Dear Lord, what had he been thinking? To kiss the sister of his life-long friends?

He hadn't been thinking, that was his problem. These possessive feelings he had for Hannah must be controlled, must be smothered before he did damage to her reputation.

To her heart.

If he were to apologize now, which he couldn't do without risking revealing their secret, it would be an insult to her. She'd likely believe he didn't want to kiss her, not that he knew the extreme impropriety he'd forced on her.

Knightwick and David would have his head. Laurence prayed they'd never hear of it. Losing their friendship would be almost as bad as losing Hannah's. The entire Lumley family would refuse to acknowledge him any more. He'd lose everyone close to him over one foolish whim. One moment's loss of self-control.

Stupid, stupid man. In a single act he'd threatened everything he held dear.

Another squeal came from the nursery above his room. All right, not everything he held dear. Yet she would be the innocent victim of any backlash that came from Laurence's actions, if anyone were to learn of it. His reputation as a rakehell would be sealed, and likely not forgotten by the time Louisa was old enough to seek a husband.

He needed to rise and go see the child, and work harder to earn her trust. And maybe consider finding a home in the country, or making the repairs the castle in Oakhurst might need, so the two of them might escape Town. It was becoming quite apparent the was not the best place for Laurence to remain.

As he sat at his dining table—another entirely new experience, breakfast in the morning, at a table—he read the morning paper, briefly skimming over the financial news to be certain his interests fared well. How odd to now be concerned about them. He had enough money to live comfortably through the longest of lifetimes and leave enough behind to see Louisa and her eventual family equally well off.

His butler paused in the doorway. "Lord Knightwick is here to see you, sir."

"Show him into my study, Gilly."

"Yes, sir."

Folding the paper and setting it on the table, Laurence drew in a deep breath. Knightwick knew about the kiss.

Knightwick stood by the bookcase, studying the titles. When he saw Laurence, he said, "You've come by quite a collection in such a short time. I never knew you to be a reader."

"I'm not. Some came with the house, and your mother ordered several she felt would improve my mind."

Smiling, Knightwick nodded. "That sounds like Mother."

"Shall I call for some coffee?" Laurence motioned to a chair before he sat behind his desk.

"No, I have errands to run. I must to speak to you on a certain matter of some urgency."

Here it came. Laurence waited for the dressing down. He was

surprised at the calm demeanor Knightwick was able to maintain, when the situation gave him leave to come to blows with no one thinking ill of him.

"Mother says you've been seen at more than a few assemblies of late."

"Yes. It would seem I'll go to any means to appear respectable." Laurence waited for the outburst.

"I was surprised to hear it. Yet it serves me well."

Was it possible Knightwick didn't know about the kiss? "How can I help you?"

"I will be away for two weeks," he said as he sat. "Mother has mentioned Lord Downham is making his attentions quite obvious, and she suspects he might not have the best of intentions."

"I've thought that very thing. In fact, I've said as much to Lady Hannah."

"You can't be seen spending an excessive amount of time with my sister, of course, but it would ease my mind if you would keep an eye on her while I am not here."

Laurence gritted his teeth to keep from laughing aloud. Knightwick had no inkling he was asking the fox to watch over the henhouse. "I'm more than happy to do so. I'd half a mind to ask you why you weren't attending the balls alongside her. Not that it's my place to tell you your duty to your sister."

"Quite so. Mother says they are to attend a theatrical at Vauxhall tonight with Lord Downham. There are too many opportunities there for Downham to take advantage of Hannah. Will you go in my place? Is there someone you might ask to accompany you with so little notice?"

"I will send a note 'round to Mrs. Turner."

Knightwick's gaze came up. "Do you think that a good choice? Given your past relationship with her? Mother might feel insulted, and will certainly think it casts a dim light on Hannah."

"No one thinks ill of Mrs. Turner when she appears at an assembly. I spoke to her recently at Lady Kettlemore's ball."

"That's quite a different situation. Regardless, I think Hannah would be suspicious of your presence if you brought Mrs. Turner among their party."

"I could escort Lady B." Laurence gave him a wry grin.

"She'd never have you." Knightwick leaned back in his chair and crossed one leg over his knee. "I am serious, Oakhurst. What have you been doing at all those balls if not meeting the young ladies?"

He wasn't going to answer that. "How can I improve my reputation if I'm seen flirting with half the ladies in the Marriage Mart and choose not to marry any of them?"

Knightwick shook his head. "I imagine it was foolish of me to think you'd know any respectable single women. Never mind. I know of one who will suit. Lady Susan Yarwood has no inclination toward marriage and her father is a friend of mine. He's been eager for her to do something other than attend her book readings. I'll make up some excuse as to why you are in need of a companion at the last minute. Perhaps I can let her in on our secret. I will tell her to expect you, Mother, and Hannah to pick her up this evening."

"I'll likely regret this," Laurence said.

He was feeling the same thing later that night as he danced with Lady Susan to the music the orchestra played. At least here at Vauxhall Gardens, there was enough room to dance without bumping into someone on each turn. He kept one eye on Hannah and Downham while speaking to Lady Susan. "Knightwick tells me you enjoy attending book readings."

"And do you disapprove?" she asked.

He had to laugh. "That wasn't the answer I expected. Not only do I not disapprove, I think you and I could be great friends."

"Oh, do you read a lot?"

"Only the papers. I had in mind your wit. Your refusal to play the demure miss. I am tired of demure misses and I've only been attending assemblies for a few weeks now."

"I would have thought Lord Knightwick would have warned you about me. He's known me since before I came out into Society. He's a good friend of my father's. They can think of nothing but their horses."

"That's Knightwick, all right." Laurence turned them closer to Hannah. At least on the dance floor Downham couldn't try anything untoward.

When the music ended, the four of them returned to the table where Lady B sat. They drank punch and the ladies fluttered their fans for a few minutes as they rested.

"The gardens are quite lovely at night, aren't they?" Lord Downham asked.

"Even more so than in the daylight, with the trees filled with lanterns," Lady B agreed.

"Would you care to stroll the paths with me, Lady Hannah?" Downham asked.

"I'd be delighted," she answered.

Laurence caught Lady B's frown. He pushed back his chair. "Excellent idea." He held his arm out to escort Lady Susan.

She rose. "Oh, yes. Such a beautiful night for it."

Hannah looked confused as she took Downham's arm, but said nothing.

Letting the other couple lead the way, Laurence stayed far enough back to give them the appearance of privacy. "This is a first for me," he admitted to Lady Susan.

"For me, also. I've attended a few musicales with Mama and Papa, but never with a gentleman, much less strolling with one in the darkness."

He motioned to the trees. "Hardly darkness. They are as well lit as any ballroom."

"Yet I've heard tales of young ladies losing their reputations on these paths."

Laurence cleared his throat. "Outspoken, aren't you? I imagine your mother hasn't heard you speak this way."

"Of course not. Don't be daft. It's rather freeing spending an evening without her, now that I think on it."

"To be honest, I'm rather surprised she let you be seen with me in such a public place."

"Knightwick assured them both you were nothing like the man you're rumored to be. As neither of them could think of an actual incident involving you and a young lady, they felt they could trust Knightwick's opinion of you."

Hannah and Downham were moving at a faster pace than Laurence and Lady Susan, and with the number of couples walking on the path, he was losing sight of them. He increased his pace a bit. "I beg your forgiveness, but I'm afraid we're falling behind."

He tried not to drag Lady Susan along as they wove between the other couples. She was such a good sport to not complain. They passed several side paths that led into darkness, and eventually he had to concede that Hannah and Downham had escaped him. He moved to the side of the path and stopped.

"Where do you think they've gone?" Lady Susan asked.

"Unless they ran down this path, they've gone down one of those other paths."

"Then we must follow."

"I can't take you away from the crowd. I don't care if you are unconcerned about your reputation, but I am." He ran a hand through his hair.

"You have little choice. If you take me back to Lady Bridgethorpe, you might arrive back here too late to prevent anything. Just the fact of our returning without them will be bad enough." She looked back the way they'd come. "Lady Hannah mentioned she hoped he would propose tonight. Perhaps that's the reason he's sought seclusion."

"A man like him doesn't seek seclusion to do the honorable thing."

"Then we must continue searching."

Laurence couldn't hide his astonishment at the girl, but there was no time to think on that. They turned down the first path they reached. Moonlight allowed them to see where they walked, but the trees were in shadow here. Lady Susan pressed closer to his arm as if the darkness frightened her. He placed his hand on top of hers where it rested on his sleeve. "Fear not. I won't compromise you."

She squeezed his arm. "It's not you I'm worried about. There could be footpads or all sorts of miscreants lurking here."

When he noticed a larger shadow than one tree should cast, Laurence slowed. "I believe that's them. Will you feel safe here while I confront them?"

"Yes, do what you must."

Fully aware he could be interrupting a pair of strangers, Laurence tried to make is footsteps loud enough to carry. He called out, "Lady Hannah? Is that you?"

She answered with what sounded like a sob.

"Hannah?" He ran the last few steps.

Downham ran away in the opposite direction. Laurence was torn between giving chase or helping Hannah, but her quiet sniffle told him which choice was the right one. He gathered her in his arms. "Are you all right?"

Hannah brought her hand to her neck and nodded. "I am now. Thank you."

"Lady Susan, will you come?" he called out.

"You brought her here? No one must see me like this." Hannah pulled away and her hands moved to her hair, her bodice, her hair again, then one hand remained pressed against the neckline of her gown.

"What did he do to you?"

"Nothing, truly. He tried, and my gown was torn when I pulled away, but what you interrupted was a disagreement, not a seduction." She sniffled again and wiped one cheek.

"A disagreement wouldn't leave you in tears." Anger burned inside him. His hands shook, itched to punch something. Someone.

Lady Susan came to Hannah's side. "You poor dear. You must pull yourself together so we may return to our table and Lady Bridgethorpe won't suspect anything."

Hannah hugged the other girl. "Mama will be so disappointed in me. I should never had allowed Downham to leave the main path."

"Did he make an offer?" Lady Susan asked.

"A request is more what I'd call it. Nothing was said of marriage." Hannah sniffled.

"I'm so sorry, you must be heartbroken."

Laurence stepped back and let the girls talk. He would swear Lady Susan had joined the crying, as her voice wavered slightly. She seemed to know just what to say to calm Hannah, though. The older girl smoothed Hannah's hair, adjusted some hairpins, and pronounced her fit for rejoining her mother. How she could see well enough to be certain Laurence wasn't sure.

They faced Laurence, and Lady Susan asked, "Shall we continue our walk?"

He held out each arm and the three of them walked in silence back to the lighted path.

When he was able to see Hannah more clearly, he cringed, and the urge to pummel Downham surged. A few of the curls had fallen from her hairstyle, making her look thoroughly kissed. The lace on her neckline was torn loose on one side.

Passersby ogled the three of them and whispered behind their hands. Laurence couldn't bring Hannah out in the main area looking this way. He remembered Lady Susan wore a shawl and realized what they must do. "Lady Susan, may Lady Hannah borrow your shawl?"

"Excellent idea." She quickly passed the garment to the other young lady.

Hannah wrapped it tightly over her shoulders.

Even having the torn garment covered didn't stop the stares. At any other time Laurence might enjoy the speculation that he'd partaken of the kisses of both young ladies, but that was before Louisa arrived in London. Before he'd begun to realize how much he cared about Hannah's reputation.

He paused just before the end of the path. Speaking softly, he said, "Lady Susan, Hannah appears to have lost a hairpin or two on our stroll. Perhaps you could assist her in repairing her appearance?"

"Of course." With minimal fuss, she straightened Hannah's appearance and they gathered their resolve to continue on as if nothing had happened. With more people about, there were surprisingly fewer stares, perhaps because there was so much more to look at.

Lady B wore a deep frown when the three of them approached. "Where have you been?" she whispered.

"We went for a stroll, Mama, as we told you."

"You seem to have lost one of your party."

Laurence helped the two young ladies into their seats. "Lord Downham suddenly determined he must leave."

"You didn't-No, I won't ask."

"To be honest, mama, I'm feeling a bit tired myself. Would you be terribly disappointed if we returned home?"

"Of course not," Lady B said. "But you must consider the others."

"I didn't want to be impolite," Lady Susan responded, "but I have had enough entertainment for one evening also."

Laurence smiled at her. He grew more impressed with her by the moment. Lady Susan had an outstanding, quick mind.

He rose. "I shall send for the carriage." This evening couldn't end soon enough. He felt awful for Hannah, knowing the questions her mother would raise. He felt worse for Hannah, with the heartbreak she'd endured. She deserved so much better than that cad, but she wouldn't have listened to anything Laurence told her on the matter.

He must call on them in the morning to be sure Hannah was recovering well.

Chapter Nine

Hannah managed to hold off her mother's questions before retiring to her room, which she did directly upon arrival. Mama must have noticed how Hannah kept the shawl wrapped so closely, but she said nothing. When Hannah looked in the mirror in her bedchamber, she saw how pink her eyes were. Mama would have noticed that, too.

When she rose the next morning, Hannah knew she must face Mama and answer her questions. She dreaded the discussion, and waited as long as she could before descending the stairs.

Mama wasn't in the dining room when Hannah entered, so she was given a small reprieve. Her relief ended quickly when a footman appeared in the doorway. "Lady Bridgethorpe requests you to join her in the morning room once you have eaten."

"Thank you, Peter." Her mouth was so dry she had to take large drinks of water between bites of her toast. She'd only eaten half of one slice when she decided she needed to speak to Mama sooner rather than later.

Her mother didn't look up from her book when Hannah entered. As she sat on the settee, Hannah said, "Good morning, Mama."

Mama placed a ribbon between the pages of her book before closing it and setting it to one side. "Did you sleep well, dear?"

"No."

"You didn't appear to have enjoyed yourself last night."

"The music and dancing were quite lovely."

"Do not play games with me. What happened on your walk with Lord Downham? Where did he disappear to?"

Hannah's eyes welled. "Oh, Mama, I was so certain he was going to ask for my hand."

"Did he ask for something else?"

"Not in so many words. He kissed me, and his hands began to caress me." Her voice cracked and she had to take a deep breath to ease the pain in her throat. "I was trapped against a tree, but managed to escape his arms just as Laurence arrived."

Surprisingly, Mama didn't react to Hannah's use of his given name. "I'm grateful he was there to protect you, although I would never have allowed you to wander away from the dancers if he or one of your brothers wasn't there."

"I was so mistaken about Lord Downham's character."

Mama sighed. "We all were, I fear. However, the Season isn't over, and you had several other suitors showing a marked interest in you. We might be able to salvage the situation in spite of this setback."

"Is that all this is to you? A 'situation'? A 'setback'? This is my life, Mama. I loved Lord Downham." Hannah wiped her eyes with her handkerchief. "I was planning our life together."

"Forgive me. I chose my words poorly." A tear ran down Mama's cheek. "I do understand. I've never had my heart broken. Your father was my only love. I hadn't realized your affections had become so strong for Lord Downham."

"To be honest, I wasn't certain myself, until I realized his true nature. I favored him above the other men, and I was ready to accept him when he asked me to marry him."

"Had he hinted he planned to?"

Hannah twisted the handkerchief in her hands. "As I understood him, I thought he was saying so. I was greatly mistaken in his intentions. Oh, Mama, what am I to do? If I was mistaken about him, how can I trust my heart with other men? I'm fond of a few others, and could possibly learn to love one. But how do I believe him capable of loving me?"

"My poor girl." Mama rushed to her side and wrapped her in a warm, heart-mending hug. "You are so loveable. There are many, many men in Town who'd love to call you wife. You needn't decide today. In fact, we can return to the country if you prefer. We can come back to Town next year, or perhaps go to Bath. There's no rush for you to marry. To be completely honest, I would prefer having you at home a bit longer. I would most prefer having you happy, however, whatever that entails."

"Thank you, Mama." Hannah let go of the pain she'd kept inside and cried on the ample, comforting shoulder of her mother's.

Later that afternoon, Hannah lay in her bed reading when Peter knocked on her door. "Miss Clawson is here. Shall I show her into the drawing room?"

"Yes. Tell her I shall be right down."

Hannah straightened her hair but didn't bother to change from her morning dress. Her friend was standing in front of the window when Hannah entered. "I'm happy to see you, Amelia."

Amelia turned and showed her frown. "You won't be when you hear what was being said at morning calls this morning."

"Oh, please tell me it isn't true. What are they saying about me?"

"The tale is different depending on the teller. Lord Downham attacked you. Lord Oakhurst attacked you. Lord Oakhurst attacked you and Lady Susan together. You and Lady Susan met with Oakhurst intentionally. Lord Oakhurst discovered you with Downham and beat the man senseless." Amelia drew in a dramatic breath. "I scarcely know what to believe, as none of it can be true."

"Actually, some of it is."

Amelia gasped. "No! Tell me."

"I walked the paths with Downham, and Laurence and Lady Susan walked behind us. Somehow we were separated, and Downham took me down a secluded path. You'll never believe the way he treated me. I thought he wanted a kiss, and I so desired to know what his kiss felt like, so I let him. He wouldn't be satisfied with just a kiss, though. If Laurence hadn't arrived when he did I fear what might have happened."

Amelia sat speechless for a few moments. "I cannot believe it of Lord Downham. It's no surprise Oakhurst came to your rescue, it's quite apparent his feelings for you. Yet I was certain Downham had those feelings, too."

"Laurence? His feelings toward me? What are you saying? He cares about me like a sister."

"I've seen how he looks at you, Hannah. That isn't brotherly love in his eyes."

Amelia must be mistaken. Surely Hannah would know if a man was in love with her.

Or perhaps not. She'd thought Downham loved her, and she couldn't have been more wrong. "In spite of what you believe, Laurence has no intentions to marry, and certainly not with me."

"I won't continue to argue with you. What does your mother say regarding all of this?"

Hannah sighed and let her shoulders slump. "She suggested we return to Bridgethorpe Manor. If what you say about the gossip is true, she might be right. I cannot be seen in Society if they are speculating over my actions with two men. And poor Lady Susan, to be dragged into my mess."

"She cares little for what Society thinks of her. Her part in any of this will be forgotten soon enough."

If only they'd forget Hannah's part in the scandal. And Laurence's. She hadn't even considered how this reflected on him, and he was working so hard to improve his standing. She was such a selfish girl to only consider her own reputation. Laurence's was so much more important now with Louisa in his care.

"It appears I will be returning to the country as soon as possible. You will write to me, won't you? Tell me of your wedding? And your wedding trip. Where do you plan to go?"

Talking of Amelia's plans lifted Hannah's spirits somewhat, and let her think of something other than the horrible man she'd believed herself in love with.

~*~

Two mornings later, Laurence was once again awakened by an early morning visit from Knightwick. He quickly pulled on some clothes and stumbled down the stairs. "Good Lord, man, don't you ever sleep?"

Knightwick sat stiffly in his chair. "I haven't slept since I received Mother's letter. I cut my trip short to return to Town. What she said made no sense. How is it both you and Downham compromised my sister in the same evening?"

Laurence sank into a chair and covered his face with his hands. "They can't believe it of her."

"I doubt people believe half of what they gossip about, but that doesn't prevent them from talking, or making the story even more entertaining. What is the truth of it? I thought you were there to protect Hannah."

Laurence explained how the night had developed, and the curious and shocked expressions they'd received when they returned to the lighted path. "I failed her. It's my fault she is in this situation."

"It's Downham's fault, not yours. Or my fault for allowing her to spend an evening with him in a place with so many avenues to misadventure."

"The talk will quiet soon, won't it? I've never paid attention to how long the stories last when they're about me." He leaned back. His anger was so great he was beyond even acting on it. He felt powerless to regain control over the situation.

He should have spoken to Lady B about his fears regarding Downham. No matter that Knightwick didn't think to mention it to her, Laurence should have done so himself.

"I don't know. No man will have anything to do with her now, though. She might not even wish to return to Town next year. By the following year there should have been enough other scandals to gossip about that Hannah will be forgotten."

Two years before she could consider finding a husband. He'd

seen how she looked when Downham was attentive. She'd be miserable with no one's flattery for so long.

She'd be close to twenty-three by then. Certainly not on the shelf, but with so many younger ladies arriving in Town each year, it would be harder to be the center of attention.

Who was he fooling? No man could fail to notice her. She was so much prettier than even the other ladies they called Diamonds. She was more sensible, and much less likely to flit from man to man than a girl in her first Season.

She didn't deserve to be hidden away. She hadn't done anything but be a victim of trusting the wrong man. Of allowing herself to be separated from her friends.

Knightwick shifted in his seat. "You're very quiet. What are you thinking?"

"I'm thinking I should marry Hannah." The words escaped him before the thought was fully formed.

His friend simply stared at him for a full minute. "You are daft. Or making a joke. Yes, that's it. You have horrible taste in humor, Oakhurst. This is a serious matter. This is my sister we are discussing. I won't stand for such ridiculous ideas."

"Why is it so ridiculous? She is fond of me, as I am of her. We get on very well. She adores Louisa. I'm in a position to take far better care of her than most any man."

"Hannah doesn't love you in the way she deserves to love her husband."

"And you're certain she wouldn't come to love me over time."

Knightwick jumped to his feet and paced the room. "I have no idea how a woman loves. I do know Hannah wishes to love a man before she marries."

"If she marries soon, the talk will die much sooner than if she simply retires to the country."

"That's true. Yet I can't agree to this. I can't agree to her marrying anyone without asking her wishes first."

"Will you let me talk to her?" Laurence held his breath waiting for an answer.

"I suppose I must. But you must promise me something."

"Yes?"

"Promise me you'll never hurt her."

"I swear to do everything in my power to be certain she is never unhappy, whether she will have me or not."

~*~

Hannah sat in the window seat in the morning room, grateful it was at the back of the house so she didn't feel as though all who passed by were peering up at the windows for a glimpse of that wicked young lady who'd disgraced herself in Vauxhall.

She and Mama would be leaving for home the next day. Mama was out paying calls on her friends, letting them know of the pending departure, and asking that they help to end the gossip. Telling the truth of the night wouldn't help, it would only label Hannah as someone foolish enough, or eager enough, to allow a man to have his way with her.

The front door opened and closed, and she assumed Mama had returned. The footsteps were too heavy for her mother, however, and a second set followed the first. Had Knightwick come?

Not having the energy to find out, Hannah remained with her forehead resting on the cool glass.

"Hannah?" Knightwick's voice came from the doorway.

"Good afternoon." She didn't turn his way.

"Hannah, Oakhurst is with me."

She turned to sit properly. "Forgive me, Lord Oakhurst. How nice of you to call. Mama is not in at the moment but I'm certain she'd welcome your visit."

Laurence walked past Knightwick. "I came to see you."

Her brother left the room, surprising Hannah to no end. He was always the first to reprimand her and Laurence when they failed to behave properly.

"Is there news about Louisa? How is she getting on with her new nursemaid?"

He walked slowly toward her. "She is well, and she enjoys the company of her nursemaid." He stopped in front of her. "I didn't come on a casual call, Hannah. After what happened a few nights past, we must consider the repercussions."

"Yes. Mama and I are leaving tomorrow. I will miss Louisa. You'll bring her the next time you come to Bridgethorpe?" Her biggest regret about leaving Town was not seeing the girl grow.

"I rather hoped you'd want to spend more time than that with her. With me."

His face softened in a way she'd never seen before. Hannah's curiosity grew.

"We've always gotten on well together. You know I care deeply for you." He looked down at his boots. "I'm not doing this well. I've never been in this situation before."

"Laurence, what are you saying?"

"I love you," he blurted out. "At first I thought I was merely jealous of another man spending his life with you, but I was wrong. I can't imagine my life without you. Please say you'll do me the honor of becoming my wife."

Her heart squeezed almost painfully. The words she'd so longed to hear just days ago. It didn't matter how much she enjoyed Laurence's company, she couldn't let him throw his life away because of her mistake. "Laurence," she said gently. "What happened between Lord Downham and myself was not your fault. You don't have to do this."

"I'm not acting out of honor. You know me better than that. I mean what I say. I want to marry you Hannah. Not to have a mother for Louisa. Not to save your reputation. Simply because I wish to share every day with you."

He looked so earnest, but she knew him too well to believe it. "I don't know how you convinced Knightwick to allow you to speak to me. I'm honored that you would offer to help me in this way, but I cannot accept your offer. You have done your duty and can free yourself of concern over my wellbeing now."

His fists clenched. "You're mistaken, Hannah. Either you misunderstand me, or you have no desire to marry me and are allowing me to retain my dignity. I will trouble you no longer. Do not be surprised if the next time you see me I ask you again. I want you for my wife, Hannah. I will love you whether we marry or not."

He spun on his heel and strode out of the room without saying good-bye.

Chapter Ten

By mid July, Hannah's misery hadn't lifted. She'd spend some weeks with Jane and Cousin Stephen, helping to care for their infant son. Of course, the child had a nursemaid and Jane was perfectly healthy, but there was some sort of magic than enveloped Hannah with she held that tiny boy in her arms.

The skin on the back of his hands was like warm silk. His lips puckered in a little bow while he slept, as though he nursed in his sleep. He was a quiet baby, so good-natured and quick to smile.

She felt she should return home, however, before she overstayed her welcome. Stephen and Jane likely wished to have time alone with just their child, enjoying their small family.

Amelia wrote that she would marry in August at her fiancé's country estate. She suggested Hannah come in the fall to see her new home. That would prove a pleasant distraction, Hannah was certain.

The only concern was what to do in the months between now and that visit.

It didn't matter that she always spent summers at Bridgethorpe Manor. Her sisters were good company, and Mama let them bathe in the pond some days, since all Hannah's brothers lived elsewhere now.

Inside her coursed a restlessness she couldn't release no matter how much she tried. Like the itch on her skin from an insect bite that could not be relieved, this inner itch was driving her mad. She walked to the village almost daily in search of a new book from the small library her father had sponsored. Rebecca, Cousin Neal's wife, was home visiting her father and on several of Hannah's visits to the village, she stopped by the vicarage to see her.

"Hannah, how good to see you," Rebecca said when Hannah called for the third time that week. "Come inside, it's awfully warm out."

"It is warm. I hadn't realized how much so when I left home." Hannah removed her bonnet and gloves in search of comfort.

"Let me fetch some lemonade. I'll join you in the drawing room in just a moment. Please make yourself comfortable."

She'd known Rebecca all her life, but since the girl was four years older than Hannah, they'd only become close when Hannah had turned fourteen. Rebecca had married Neal the previous year and they'd moved to a home Neal bought. As hard as it'd been for Hannah to say good-bye to her friend, she was beyond excited that Rebecca had found love.

Rebecca carried in two glasses of lemonade. "Here we are. This will help put you to rights." After handing one to Hannah, she took her place in the worn, comfortable chair by the window. "How are your sisters? Any news to pass on?"

"So little happens, I'm bored silly. What did we used to do to pass our time in the heat of summer?"

"Surely it's not as bad as all that."

"I imagine not." Hannah took a sip of the sweet yet tart drink.

"You've told me what led to your departing London before most of the others went to their country homes. Is that all that's bothering you? Having spoken of it should make you more comfortable, so there must be something you're hiding."

"Not hiding, exactly. You're too dear to me to do so. I didn't tell you the entire story. You see, after embarrassing myself so horribly at Vauxhall, my brothers' friend Lord Oakhurst-you knew him as Mr. Pierce-asked me to marry him."

"I recall him being so very pleasant company. Why didn't

you accept his offer? You obviously didn't hate the idea of leaving home, with as unhappy as you are to be here now."

Hannah took the end of the ribbon tied around her waist and slipped it through her fingers. "I fear he proposed out of feelings of guilt. He's so protective of me. He felt he'd let my family down by not preventing Downham from kissing me."

"I can believe that of him. He used to keep your brothers from teasing you quite often when you were little."

"He did, didn't he? He's my personal Lancelot, I imagine."

Rebecca raised an eyebrow. "Or is he King Arthur, the faithful, strong and loving husband? Lancelot coveted a woman who wasn't free to come to him. Lord Oakhurst would never do such a thing."

Laughing, Hannah said, "You always manage to turn stories into parables. Regardless which character I liken him to it doesn't change the fact that, had Downham not compromised me, Laurence wouldn't have proposed."

"I wonder…"

"You can wonder all you care to, but since he's already done so, it's pointless."

Rebecca swirled the remaining liquid in her glass, watching the movement. "I take it from your lack of excitement, not to mention the fact you neglected to tell me about the proposal until now, you turned him down."

"Yes. I don't want a husband who isn't in love with me. Madly, passionately in love with me. I see no other way for a happy life together."

"You'll find your perfect man. I'm certain of it. Perhaps you'll meet someone passing through the village here, just like I met Neal."

"I don't think I want a different husband. As much as I keep insisting I'm not marrying, I spend an excess of time thinking of Laurence."

"He's quite handsome. I see no reason to stop mentioning him at every turn."

Hannah laughed again. "You are so good for me. I just hope I can find someone I could love as well as I did Laurence. It's a lot to ask for, but stranger things have been done.

~*~

Laurence's day became so much brighter when he drew near Bridgethorpe Manor late one afternoon in August. Louisa slept on the opposite bench, her head in her nursemaid's lap. The puppy lay on the other side of the bench, also sleeping.

He was too restless to sleep. He hadn't slept well since they'd left Town. This visit was the first since David and Joanna's wedding the year before. With David living in Newcastle, there was no reason for Laurence to call on the family.

No reason until now. He was making good on his words to Hannah.

When the carriage rolled to a stop in front of the magnificent estate house, Louisa sat up and rubbed her eyes. "Are we there?"

"Yes, this is our destination. We'll stay for several days, I hope. You might even get to ride on a pony while we're here." He shouldn't make promises he couldn't be certain to keep, but they always rode through the fields when he visited. Louisa was old enough to sit on a pony and learn to at least walk in a small circle.

The butler came out to greet the carriage, placing a step below the door. Laurence held Louisa's arm out for the man to help her down, then descended himself.

"Was your trip pleasant, Lord Oakhurst?" The graying butler had been with the family as long as Laurence could remember.

"Yes, the weather remained clear the entire trip."

"Very good, your lordship. Lady Bridgethorpe is awaiting you in the drawing room." He turned and led the way.

Lady B set aside her needlework and smiled warmly. "How delightful of you to come. And to bring Louisa. I've missed her so."

He chuckled. "With the number of your children still at home you could hardly have a moment to think of any others."

"You understand so completely, especially for a man who was an only child. Have your nursemaid take your ward to the nursery and I'll ring for a footman to take up some biscuits and milk for her."

"Thank you."

Before he could turn away, she spoke again. "I'm aware of the reason for your visit, even though you didn't say anything specific in your letter."

"I see. And do you approve?"

"It's not my place to approve or disapprove. You may speak to Lord Bridgethorpe about the matter, and if he approves, only then may you speak to Hannah. Is that understood?"

"Yes, ma'am." He felt as if he were ten years old again, standing before her with Adam and David on his first visit. She'd been so threatening, so stern, and the attention made him love her all the more.

Lord Bridgethorpe was napping, so Laurence went to his bedchamber to splash some water on his face. While riding in the carriage didn't allow dust to reach him, he always felt dirty after a long trip.

He was no longer given one of the smaller rooms on the same floor as the nursery, being treated as an adult in recent years. The bed in his chamber was large with curtains hanging from the four posts. It could easily have been in the house since it's creation, how ever many years ago that had been.

The sight of the bed pulled at him, causing visions of the family he one day hoped to have. It would only happen if Hannah agreed to it, though. In the months since he'd seen her last, he'd come to that realization.

Hannah was the only woman he could ever love.

Shortly before supper, Laurence was taken to Lord Bridgethorpe's study to see the man. "Your lordship, you are looking well."

"Thank you, Oakhurst. You are as well. To what do we owe this visit?"

"I'm here about Lady Hannah. I wish to ask her to marry me."

Lord Bridgethorpe frowned. "I was given the impression you'd done so and been turned down. Do you truly wish to risk asking her again? I'd hate to have you so uncomfortable you no longer wish to visit us."

"I told her I would speak to her when she'd had time to recover from her unfortunate incident." He wouldn't go into the details he was certain Lord B. already knew.

"I imagine it can't hurt to let you see her, then. I shall have her meet you in the library."

"Thank you, sir." Laurence bowed his head and went to the library.

He would swear hours passed before Hannah appeared. She seemed years older, more mature than when he'd last seen her in Town. He wanted to throttle Downham for stealing the joy from her eyes. "Lady Hannah, I'm pleased you will speak with me."

"Did you fear I no longer wished to see you? I told you, you will always be special to me. As a brother, of course."

He swallowed the lump of dread in his throat that threatened to cut off his air. "I remember your words. And if you'll recall, I said I'd speak to you once more on a certain subject, and if it was still too unpleasant for you to consider, I'd never bring up the matter again."

He didn't wait for her to respond. "I told you in June how much I loved you, and since then I've only grown to love you more. I'm not saying this because I feel guilty over what happened. I wish I'd spoken before we ever visited Vauxhall Gardens. Would you have trusted me to speak from the heart then?"

Hannah's lips turned down. "At that point I still considered myself in love with another man. I wouldn't have considered your suit as I was waiting for his."

"Do you trust me now with the truth?"

"I do. You've only reaffirmed what I've always known about you. You're honest, protective, and a great joker. You care about family. You care about justice. I admire you greatly, Laurence."

"You sound as though the next thought begins with, 'But…'"

She grinned. "But…we know too much about each other to make for a happy marriage?" she asked.

"I disagree. We know enough about ourselves to know we'd succeed at a happy life together."

She smiled but said nothing.

"I won't spout flowery words for you this time, Hannah. You know what I'm asking. Marry me. Share my life, my heart."

"Since arriving home I've thought often about what you said to me in June. I've begun to accept that you might truly love me. You know me better than anyone, and yet here you are asking for my hand again. How can I believe anything else?"

"Then may I have your answer?"

"Yes. My answer is yes, Laurence. I love you. I misjudged it to be like what I feel for my brothers, but as I said, I've thought about us almost constantly in the past two months. You are the only man I can be my true self around. I can't imagine marrying anyone else."

"Are you certain?" He was frozen in his spot.

"You've waited two months to hear my answer and this is all you can say to me?"

"I'm unable to find words." Now he took the steps that brought him close to her. He stroked one of her cheeks, his fingers noticeably warm against her cool skin. Trailing a finger beneath her jaw, he lifted her face and lowered his lips to hers.

He savored her minty taste, the soft pressure of her lips against his. He would never get enough of kissing her. "I love you, Hannah. With all my heart, all my being. I will work every day of my life to keep you happy."

"If you work every day I'll never see you, and that would make me very unhappy. I love you, dear man. I'll be forever grateful to Louisa for bringing us together. I'll treat her as my own child, if that's all right with you."

He nodded, resting his head on hers. "I think you've been doing that since first you met. That act alone has made her transition so much easier. I hope you'll always feel that way about her."

She stood on her toes and kissed him again. "How can I not? She reminds me of you in many ways."

"Lord help us when she turns eighteen, then. I doubt I could survive a Season with someone as wild as me."

He'd do it, though. He would endure any number of Seasons in the future to be allowed to show off this beautiful woman on his arm. He'd come so close to never having her. She loved him. He was very blessed.

I hope you enjoyed Her Impetuous Rakehell. Please continue reading this excerpt from my Civil War novella, The Lieutenant's Promise.

The Lieutenant's Promise

Chapter One

June 28, 1861
Wilson Creek, Missouri

"Cletus Bocephus Gilmore, you get your tail back here before I tan your hide." Emily Gilmore waved a switch at the enormous hog that'd escaped his pen yet again. It had plenty of mud available to keep itself cool, thanks to the unrelenting rain this past week. The sun managed to break through this morning just long enough to make the air thick and heavy, but not dry the ground.

Cletus ignored her shouts and continued to waddle toward the woods on the edge of Em's family's farm. This had become almost a ritual, his knocking down a fence rail and slipping out to rut his way through the fresh undergrowth in the woods on the west end of the farm. Although, slipping wasn't the best word to use on a critter his size.

"Em, wait," cried Billy from behind.

She paused and glanced back at her little brother. The poor boy had a smudge of dirt in his sandy brown hair already. He was always forgetting to wear his hat. At eight, he was finally old enough to take on a few of the chores more difficult than gathering eggs or slopping the pigs. Try as he might, it didn't make up for the fact that Tom, ten years older than Billy and four younger than Em's twenty-two, had just joined up with the Union Army after the secessionists took over the governmental buildings in Jefferson City.

Ma was beside herself now with worries. After Pa died, Tom had taken on much of the heavy work that now fell to Em, and Ma was certain Em couldn't keep the farm going. Ma had her hands full with the younger kids, and hadn't been herself since Harvey's birth almost two years ago. Having lost her husband six months before didn't help.

Em watched Billy struggle to pull his boot out of the mud, wobbling on his other foot. She walked back, bent down and tugged the boot free, noticing the mud beginning to clump on the hem of her dress. "There you go. Now let's get that boar and put him back in his pen. We have chores to do."

Rufus, the old red hound, had his nose to the ground and ran off after whatever animal he'd smelled.

Once Cletus found the tender shoots he sought and ate enough to feel indulged, he allowed Em and Billy to guide him back. As the three of them trekked between the trees, through the briars, and around the stumps, Em heard movement to their left. She grabbed Billy's arm and raised a finger to her lips.

Billy nodded, looking in the direction of the footfalls. Cletus continued on his way, filling the quiet with his satisfied grunts.

Em crouched and Billy did the same. She heard voices now, but they weren't close enough to make out their words.

Billy looked over his shoulder at her. "It's Tom," he whispered.

"How can you tell? I can't see a thing."

"I know his voice."

She shook her head, still unable to make out anything more than the fact they spoke casually, no sense of urgency. That was a good sign, perhaps. After the battle near Boonville to the north, she worried that the Missouri State Guardsmen would ride through their area, recruiting men to fight on the side of the secessionists. It wasn't likely, with the Union soldiers said to be at one of the forts not far from Springfield, but with Pa in his grave and Tom gone, the protection of her family fell to her.

The voices drew closer, and Em heaved a sigh. "You're right, Billy. That's Tom. I should've listened to you. Come on."

She rushed toward the approaching figures. "Tom! What are you doing here?"

"I live here, remember?" He winked at her. He stopped in front of her, setting the butt of his rifle on the toe of his boot, likely to keep it out of the mud. His dark brown hair stuck out beneath his dark blue Union cap. Tom looked so grown up in his uniform. It was hard to think of him as a man now. He was still the brat who used to tug her pigtails and push her down in the pigpen.

A handsome, slightly taller young man, also in uniform, chuckled beside Tom. His straight, brown hair needed a trim, but it simply gave him a more rugged look that belied his crisp military stance. He grinned, sending her pulse racing. The dimple in his left cheek certainly added to his charm, as did the light of laughter in his deep brown eyes.

She tore her gaze away from him to chide her brother. "Don't be daft. Why aren't you with the rest of the troop?" Panic suddenly hit, her stomach knotting. "Have the rebels come this far?"

"That's what we're here to find out," the stranger said.

"Lieutenant Lucas, this is my sister, Emily. Em, this is Lieutenant Levi Lucas."

"It's a pleasure, Miss Gilmore." He bowed slightly, like a gentleman, making her wonder where he was from. His accent said Missouri, but few men she knew locally had fine manners like his.

"You find us on reconnaissance," he continued. "Our company is camped a few miles north of here, so you might see Union soldiers passing through. No need to alarm yourself."

"That tells me you believe the rebels are here." She studied his face. He was probably keeping anything he knew to himself, either to prevent her from being afraid for her family's safety, or to stop her from saying something to the wrong people.

The lieutenant raised one eyebrow. "If we knew where they were, we wouldn't be searching, now would we?"

Emotion heated her skin, but Em wasn't sure if it was embarrassment or outrage. The nerve of the man speaking as if she were a child, or a simpleton. Lifting her head and straightening her shoulders, she spoke in an equally polite voice. "I'd have thought the Union Army was better organized than to send its men out willy-nilly. Forgive my ignorance."

The right side of Lieutenant Lucas's mouth twitched and he appeared to be fighting a smile. "Touché, Miss Gilmore. You do, however, understand the need to keep our maneuvers closely guarded. The Missouri State Guard fled south after their defeat at Boonville, that much is true."

Em glanced at Tom, and back at the lieutenant. "Do I need to take the rifle with me when I leave the house? And insist Billy stay behind? What about Maggie working the fields with me? Will she be safe?"

"I don' wanna stay by the house, Em," Billy argued. "Ma said I'm big enough to help with chores now. Besides, I can shoot almost as well as you."

That much was true, she hated to say. Even Maggie was a better shot than Em was. She waited for Tom to answer.

"Yes, take the rifle. I don't think we'll have raids like in the border wars, do you think, Lieutenant?"

"I pray we don't. Those raids wrought terror on innocent people. The Missouri State Guard should be more organized in their fighting. At least, they've proven themselves to be. To this point, they've only challenged Union troops, not civilians." He lifted the brim of his cap, gazing down at Em with a serious expression. "Be alert, Miss Gilmore. You can never tell how passionate men might behave."

Her heart fluttered as she took his words to mean something else entirely. She could easily imagine him threatening to steal a kiss…would she put up a fight?

Stop that! The man talked of battles and killings, but she could only think of love. It was a nice diversion from the next chore needing her attention.

Chores. Remembering why she'd gone to the woods, she searched for their boar. "Cletus. We were chasing him back to his pen." She ran off toward the farm.

Heavy footfalls sounded behind her, then Tom passed her by. "I should fix those posts before we move on," he called back.

"I can do it," she argued. "You are on duty, aren't you?"

The Lieutenant caught up to them. "If the two of us work together, we can have it done quickly enough. You'd best keep the pig contained and stay out of the woods."

For some reason, his words angered her. He thought she knew nothing about safety. She had more than enough to worry about with coyotes and bobcats in the nearby woods, and the fox that loved to steal their chickens.

To keep from saying something she'd regret, she slowed and waited for Billy to catch up. "You're getting pretty fast," she encouraged when he reached her side.

"No, I'm not. My legs aren't as long as yours."

Em smiled. He was too old already to be treated like a child. Thank goodness Susie and Harvey would stay young a while longer.

Cletus was nosing about the picket fence surrounding the vegetable garden, but he was easily led through the gate of his pen. Tom showed Lieutenant Lucas where the fence posts were stacked, while he went into the shed for hammers and nails.

Before returning to her chores, Em spoke to Billy. "Go tell Ma Tom stopped by. She'll want to see him."

Fred, their mule, was still tied to the tree where she'd left him when Cletus escaped. Hitching the plow to the mule, she started at one corner of the field where they'd just harvested the early corn. Fred worked with little complaint, which made the job much easier.

In the middle of the field, as she turned back toward the barn, she noticed the lieutenant watching her with his hand held beyond the brim of his cap, shading his eyes. If they were done with the fence, shouldn't they be getting on their way? Lieutenant Lucas remained in place the closer she came to him.

"Whoa, Fred." Em wiped her hand where her bonnet rested on her forehead before the dampness could reach her eyes. "You two finished the pig pen fence?"

"We did," he said.

She gnawed the inside of her cheek to keep away a smile. "You didn't happen to shovel the pen out while you were there, did you?"

He glanced down at his uniform. "I'm sure you can tell by looking at me. I remained outside the pen while we worked. Tom has spare clothes here. I'd have to wear that stench until we return to camp tonight. How am I supposed to conceal my presence when they can smell me coming from miles away?"

"Stay downwind?" She bit her lip, holding in laughter. He still looked so polished, and her hem had to be six inches deep in mud by now. Plowing after a rainy spell meant having her boots gain three pounds each by the time she finished a field, even when she waited a few days for the land to dry out some. She had to sit on the porch at the end of the day and scrape her boots, and take them off before going inside.

What must he think of her, wearing the farm from head to toe as she must be, rather than poised and perfumed as the ladies he was likely accustomed to? What bothered her more than his opinion of her appearance was her concern over it.

He glanced out over the fields and outbuildings, his hands resting on his hips. "You are working land this on your own?"

"My sister helps me. Our hand, Jasper, is a freeman, and he moved north. He was afraid of what might happen to him and his family with the secessionists causing so much trouble." His concern rubbed her the wrong way. He and Tom faced much more danger than her family.

"There's no one living nearby that you can ask for help?"

"Come harvest time in the fall, several of the families get together and help each other."

He shook his head, rubbing the back of his neck. "It's not safe for you here, not without a man around."

Her fists began to clench, and she debated walking away to end the conversation. "We don't have much choice in the matter, until Tom is able to come home for good."

"Your farm is on the path between the Union camps and the likely position of the Home Guard. The next battle could fall right here in your fields. Where will you go to escape the cannons and gunfire?"

Em leaned forward to be certain he heard every word. "There's the basement, a root cellar in the barn, and the springhouse. We've kept safe from tornadoes that have passed close by. We can do the same when we hear gunfire."

His lips thinned, but he said nothing.

Her patience was at its end. "If you're that concerned, perhaps you'd better make certain the secessionists don't come near the farm."

His eyes widened. He straightened as though he were standing at attention.

Standing there arguing with him wasn't getting her work done. "I'd best get back to it." She reined the mule into a turn and straightened the plow.

Lieutenant Lucas walked toward her. "Wait. If we've delayed ourselves this long, we can stay a little longer, assuming we aren't seen by anyone from my company. Let me do that for you."

She halted Fred, glancing at the lieutenant's boots. "I thought you were concerned about your uniform."

"The mud doesn't bother me. The pig's…er, stench, does."

"Well then, if you're certain." She lifted the looped reins over her head and offered them to him. "You put this behind your back, then hold-"

"Yes, I've done this before." He positioned himself behind the plow and went to work.

With her hands on her hips, and her jaw slightly ajar, Em watched him walk away. This Lieutenant Lucas was a most intriguing man.

Tom came to stand beside her, wiping his hands on a kerchief. "What's he up to now?"

"That's obvious."

Shaking his head, Tom said, "We need to move on. We won't cover enough territory."

Ma came out with two jars of lemonade, and offered one to Tom. "Why is your friend working while you stand here lollygagging?"

"I worked, Ma. I put up some new fence posts in Cletus's pen."

"With the lieutenant's help, or so Billy told me." Ma's voice was sharp. "Now you put him to work in the field. Didn't I raise you better than that?"

"He volunteered," Em said. "Tom didn't have the chance to offer before Lieutenant Lucas had the reins."

"I was tellin' Em we need to get back to scoutin'," Tom said.

"I should get something else done since he's helping out." Em left them arguing and hustled to the barn. She didn't need Ma jumping on her for standing around doing nothing. It wasn't as though she had the chance to do so very often, but she'd regret it later, when she looked at all the chores awaiting her still.

~*~

Levi stepped to either side of the furrow as he plowed. It'd been several years since he worked his grandfather's farm and he'd forgotten how much effort it took keeping the plow upright. His sisters would never be able to finish half a field in a day, much less the entire one, as Miss Gilmore obviously could.

In the evenings after their drills in camp, Tom spoke often about his older sister, whom he admired immensely. He hadn't mentioned how pretty she was, nor how sassy. The word bossy came to mind as he tried to recall Tom's descriptions.

Levi smiled. She was quite bossy at that. Being the eldest child on a farm almost ensured it, especially when their father had died. Miss Gilmore and Tom probably split the chores after his death. The next younger sister most likely took on Tom's share when he enlisted.

His mind continued to wander until he reached the end of the field. Glancing at the sky, Levi realized how much of the day they'd spent on chores rather than reconnaissance. They'd have to hurry to cover enough territory before sundown. Yet he couldn't have walked away leaving Miss Gilmore behind the plow.

He wasn't able to be there everyday to take on her heavy work, but he could relieve her of a few hours' worth.

Levi led the mule under a tree to wait in the shade while he looked for Miss Gilmore to see if there was more land to plow. He found her in the barn sharpening an axe. "I left the mule harnessed to the plow. Do you have more fields to do today?"

Em straightened, pressing a hand to her back. "Thank you for your help. I'll take care of him."

He stepped between her and the barn door. "I didn't mean to leave more work for you."

"You relieved me of a large portion of the chores. I can't ask for more. Not when you two are supposed to be on duty. You'd best find Tom and be on your way." She smiled and moved past him. "Where'd you learn to plow?"

"On my grandfather's farm." His longer stride had him beside her in two steps, unwilling to leave her just yet. She intrigued him. "Perhaps if we have leave, I could come visit with Tom." He held his breath as he waited for her answer.

She peered up at him from beneath the brim of her bonnet. "Do you men get leave often? Aren't you needed in case the rebels return?"

"They were headed to Arkansas, from what we've been told. I doubt they'll be back. Not with General Lyon in control of Jefferson City."

She didn't pause as she reached the mule and untied his reins from the tree branch. "I thought you were concerned for our safety because of how close the State Guard was. Well, you're welcome to call on our family anytime you're in the area." Her smile grew and she tossed him a sly glance. "Especially if you care to take on a few chores."

"I might just do that."

"I believe you would. I can see how you earned your rank, Lieutenant Lucas."

"I'll go find Tom, and be on our way. It was a pleasure to meet you."

"And you, too."

Tom was just hammering the last nail in a board on the porch when Levi found him. "There you are," Tom said. "Next time you decide to flirt with my sister, warn me so I don't get put to work."

"Your absence is part of the reason that work is undone." Levi raised a hand to ward off any indignation. "I understand why you enlisted, it's likely the same reason I did. To keep your family safe, protect the state from what was happening in Kansas. I was working on my grandfather's farm when the town of Lawrence was overrun and burned. My cousin was killed just walking down the road. It's bad enough when some want to continue to own slaves, but destroying homes and cities and killing innocent people is beyond the pale."

Tom didn't respond until he'd put away his tools and said goodbye to his family. As they walked down the road away from Springfield, he squinted into the sun. "I was torn when we heard what happened in Boonville. The border wars between the loyalists here in Missouri and the free-staters in Kansas were bad, but they were far enough away I could pretend my family was safe."

"Pretending is easy to do, at least for a short time."

"Exactly. We've never owned slaves, but we've never spoke out against them, either. Pa didn't want to stir up trouble, so he said to walk away from any discussions." He spat on the dirt road. "Maybe if we'd spoken out like we should have, if more people like us had, we wouldn't be fighting over slavery now."

"Or, you might have been killed like my cousin. You wouldn't help your family at all that way. At least in the army you can help change things."

"Yeah, but that leaves all the work to the girls."

"And your mother."

"No, Ma hasn't been well since Harvey was born. She never got her strength back. Even bringing water from the well tires her out."

That left a lot of work for the two older sisters, with their hired hand gone. They needed Tom back.

Watching over the safety of the men in his company was a part of Levi in everything he did. Seeing exactly what the loss of his friend would do to Tom's family made him double up on that vow to see that Tom made it home when his enlistment was up.

About The Author

USA Today Bestselling Author Aileen Fish is an avid quilter and auto racing fan who finds there aren't enough hours in a day/week/lifetime to stay up with her "to do" list. There is always another quilt or story begging to steal away attention from the others. When she has a spare moment she enjoys spending time with her two daughters and their families, and her fairy princess granddaughter. Her books include The Bridgethorpe Brides series and the Small Town Sweethearts series.

Stay up to date with book releases at her website http://aileenfish.com or on https://www.facebook.com/AileenFishAuthor

Other Books By Aileen Fish

Excerpts and buy links are available at <u>http://aileenfish.com/books.</u>
<u>html</u>

Regency Romance Novellas

A Bride for Christmas
The Mistletoe Mishap
The Viscount's Sweet Temptation
Her Secondhand Duke
A Pretense of Love
Helena's Christmas Beau

The Bridgethorpe Brides Series (Regency)

His Impassioned Proposal
The Incorrigible Mr. Lumley
Charming the Vicar's Daughter
Her Impetuous Rakehell
One Last Season
Captivated by the Wallflower (in Sweet Summer Kisses)
Chasing Lord Mystery
Captain Lumley's Angel (in Beaux, Ballrooms and Battles)

Love's Promises series (Victorian America)
The Lieutenant's Promise
A Lasting Promise (Fall 2015)
A Christmas Promise (Winter 2016)

Anthologies

A Christmas Courtship
Regency Christmas novellas: *The Viscount's Sweet Temptation, A Bride for Christmas,* and *The Mistletoe Mishap.*

The Heart of a Duke
Includes *Her Secondhand Duke* and four connected Regency Romance stories centering around five girlfriends in search of love.

Sweet Christmas Kisses
14 Sweet Christmas Kisses, a bundle of G- and PG-rated contemporary romance novels and novellas from USA Today, national bestselling, and award-winning authors. Includes *Christmas in White Oak.*

Beaux, Ballrooms and Battles
A Celebration of Waterloo. 9 Regency romance novellas of love tested by war. Includes *Captain Lumley's Angel.*

To Love a Spy
A collection of wickedly suspenseful and wildly charming historical romances with bold heroes and dauntless heroines who must use unconventional methods to deliver justice—and hopefully find a love that proves a perfect fit for their hearts. Includes *The Lieutenant's Promise.*

Sweet Summer Kisses
Wallflowers and bluestockings have their chance at love. Includes *Captivated by the Wallflower.*

Contemporary Romance

The Small Town Sweethearts Series

Cowboy Cupid
The Cowgirl and the Geek
Christmas in White Oak

Young Adult

Cat's Rule (In the anthology Wild at Heart Volume II)
Outcast (Apocalyptia Book One)

Paranormal

The Lives of Jon McCracken (print and ebook)

Manufactured by Amazon.ca
Bolton, ON

29210599R00061